THE CHOLO TREE

THE CHOLO TREE

DANIEL CHACÓN

PIÑATA
BOOKS

PIÑATA BOOKS
ARTE PÚBLICO PRESS
HOUSTON, TEXAS

The Cholo Tree is funded in part by grants from the City of Houston through the Houston Arts Alliance, the National Endowment for the Arts and the Texas Commission on the Arts. We are grateful for their support.

Piñata Books are full of surprises!

Arte Público Press
University of Houston
4902 Gulf Fwy, Bldg 19, Rm 100
Houston, Texas 77204-2004

Cover design by Victoria Castillo
Cover photograph by Marina Tristán

Cataloging-in-Publication (CIP) Data for *The Cholo Tree* is available.

Printed in the United States of America
May 2017–June 2017
Versa Press, Inc., East Peoria, IL

7 6 5 4 3 2 1

37123000854445

DEDICATION

This novel was the most difficult book for me to write, to continue to write, to enter into every day for about five years, after which I let it sit for another five years, and went back into it again. There were so many times I wanted to give up, not because I didn't love the character, but because the voice in my head kept saying, "Why are you writing about a cholo? Nobody wants to hear the story of a cholo!"

But I kept writing because the protagonist of the story kept asserting his voice, saying to me, "I'm not a cholo. I'm an artist."

I think he really believed what he was saying to me, and if this sounds strange, ask any fiction writer, the characters take on personalities of their own, and they surprise you.

The great Argentine writer Jorge Luis Borges said if the writer isn't surprised about what happens in his fiction, neither will the reader be surprised.

My character, in *The Cholo Tree*, Victor, convinced me he wasn't a cholo, but I think he was convincing himself. Maybe there was something in him, some deep root that suggested he was a branch on this particular cultural tree.

And although I didn't set out to write about a cholo, I love this character, and just because people stereotype the urban Chicano doesn't mean I should stay away from writing about them with love and understanding.

So I dedicate this book to all the cholos in my life, the cholos I love and respect and the cholos that I only brushed against socially for a brief periods of time.

I especially dedicate this book to my two favorite cholos, my brother the poet Kenneth Robert Chacón and my cousin Andrew Calderon.

I love you guys.

You are my greatest dogs.

And to all the other cholos who maybe don't even know they're cholos, but everyone else thinks they are and everybody else pigeonholes them so that it becomes easier to act the way people expect them to.

To all the cholos in la Chicanada, with love.

PART ONE
MY FIRST DEATH

I died when I was fourteen years old.

Not many people could say that, but legally I was dead, and then the doctors said I somehow came back to life. I thought Jessica would ask me all kinds of questions, like did I see my father, or was Jesus there to greet me, or was there a great light that I was walking into. But all she did when she picked me up from the hospital was say, "Get in the car, *menso!*"

As she drove, she shoved her arm inside her big ol' purse and started searching for something. "Do you know what a stereotype you are?" she asked. "You're the existential Chicano."

She pulled out a package of Wrigley's Spearmint gum. She unwrapped a stick and put it in her mouth.

"I mean the Quinn Essential Chicano. That's what you are. It means you're typical. I took that Chicano literature class at City, and I'll tell you right now, your story is so old."

She said "so" as if it had two syllables.

"No one wants to hear it no more," she said. "Nobody cares about you no more."

"No more? How can you talk about existential Chicano in one sentence and then use double negatives in another?"

She gave me a mad-dog look. "Don't start on that."

She chewed her gum as if she were angry at it and wanted it to suffer. "Menso," she said. "My professor told us that Chicano literature isn't even called Chicano literature no more, and you know why? Because the rest of us don't give a damn about you *cholos*. You're a disgrace to our people. You take us back to when men beat women as if they were garbage."

"I'm not a cholo."

"Why don't you want to change your ways? Why don't you want to get better? I mean, *¡Ay Dios mío!* You almost died! No, you *did* die. They told me you were dead!"

"Sorry to disappoint you."

"I can't believe I trusted you. I'm the *mensa* for believing in you."

"I'm not a cholo," I repeated, more for me than for her, because I knew she wasn't listening to me. I started to wonder why so many adults thought I was a thug, which is what she had meant by "cholo."

Maybe it was my age. I was fourteen years old, and a lot of old people didn't trust teenagers. Maybe it was the way I walked. Maybe it was my Oakland Raiders T-shirt. Whatever it was, most adults, white or Mexican, assumed I was a gang member or that I was on the verge of becoming one. Whenever Equis and I went into malls, security followed us around, and sometimes city police stopped and frisked us against their cars.

I didn't go around looking for fights, and I didn't get drunk or do meth. I didn't go to cholo parties, and practically every kid on the (oh-so-stereotypical) East Side of town where I lived dressed like I did. But not all of them were hassled about being in a gang.

I'm brown.

I mean, dark-chocolate brown.

I have a wide, Indian nose and bushy eyebrows. I was convinced that most adults were basically racist. Even the old Mexicans preferred the light-skinned Hispano over the *indio* Chicano, and I was as indio as they came.

One time a teacher told me if I ever wanted to be anyone in life, I had to get that chip off my shoulder.

"What chip?" I asked.

"The whole world isn't against you," she said.

"Against me?"

"You have nothing to rage against."

I had no idea what she was talking about. It's true I didn't care about school, because it was boring and I got bad grades. And maybe I did a few things I wasn't supposed to do, like smoke pot and sell a little on the side, but how does that make me an angry, young man?

Anyway, this particular teacher, a mousey woman, was Hispanic.

"It's not like there hasn't been progress for our people," she said. "If you know what I mean."

And no, I had no idea what she meant until later, when I realized she wasn't looking at some Hispanic boy who liked to draw; she was looking at a cholo.

※ ※ ※

One time in Social Studies, Mr. Beasley was having a discussion about the origins of street gangs. He said they were started for a good purpose, to provide protection for people in neighborhoods that cops didn't care about protecting. "Even today," he said, "all gang members are not bad people."

The students grumbled, some in agreement and some in disagreement. Our school was about 100 percent people of color: Chicanos, Blacks, Assyrians, Southeast Asians, all of us poor kids from the inner city.

"Victor," said Mr. Beasley. "You're a decent guy, aren't you? I can tell, you're a good kid."

"You see right through me, Mr. Beasley," I said.

"See?" he said to the class.

I liked Mr. Beasley, so I didn't bother telling him that I wasn't a gang member, which turned out to be a mistake. He submitted my name for a teach-in on gang violence.

They called it "Gang Awareness Day," and they wanted to get all the gang leaders together for a "positive dialogue." I was in my third-period English class. A Hmong lady came into the class with a clipboard, called my name and told me to come with her. I followed her down the hall, turning the corner into another hallway, past a big room with books and then another hallway with a door at the end. We entered a room where chairs were put in a circle. Sitting in those chairs, like stereotypes from every movie ever made about gangs in the schools were the hardest looking kids you could imagine. It scared me, really, to be honest. I swallowed and must have contracted my entire body, my fists curling, the snakes on my forehead arching for the attack. I took a seat, and like the rest of the boys, I stretched my legs and crossed my arms, as if I were too cool to sit in such a silly chair.

There were Black gangs, Cambodian gangs, Vietnamese gangs, Hmong, Assyrian and, of course, the "Hispanic" gang represented by yours truly.

I was kind of scared that all these leaders might think I was in a gang. But it turned out a lot of us weren't real bangers, we just looked like it to school authorities. There was an Asian kid, looked angry, his eyes squinted at everything he looked at, and he wore baggy pants, a white huge T-shirt with nothing on it and red Nikes untied.

During the break, one of the Black "gangsters" asked me, "Why they got you here?"

"They're stupid," I said and he laughed and said, "Got that right."

He was tall and thin and had clear eyes. "I'm Boot," he said. He lifted his hand for me and we brushed our fingers together like cool, minority kids.

"Victor," I said.

For the rest of the day we hung out, laughing at stuff together. We even had lunch together. As we watched the other bad-ass kids, I asked him if he was really in a gang or if they just stereotyped him.

"It's all good," he said, shrugging his shoulders.

Even now, on the way home from the hospital, where even the doctors thought I was a goner, my mom looked over at me and shook her head in disgust or anger or both. I knew she wasn't seeing me. She wasn't looking at Victor Reyes, a boy who loved to draw, who wanted some day to be as successful as the cartoonist Lalo Alcaraz, who liked the TV series *Weeds*, who was the only living child of her dead husband, no, she wasn't seeing me. Who was she seeing?

"See? This is the problem," she said. "You're never home."

We were driving down Belmont Avenue, right through the barrio, past minimarts and used car lots. "You're always on the streets with your 'homies,' those *ratones*. You have no discipline."

"You work fourteen hours a day," I said. "My entire summer vacation all I do is stay home. I mean, I go out during the day sometimes with Equis, but everyone needs to get out of the house once in a while or they'll go crazy!"

"What were you doing fighting those boys, Victor? Why were you fighting them? Why did they attack you so badly? You must have done something. That kind of anger can't be random."

When I woke up from what the doctors called legal death, I had lost my recent memory, which was most of that summer. I didn't know why I was killed in a fight. I didn't know how I ended up in the parking lot of the Cherry Auction, or how I got to the hospital.

"Why were you fighting those boys?" she demanded.

"I don't know, but my point is that you're never home to notice I'm usually home. Who do you think keeps the apartment clean?"

I was the only one who ever cleaned. I was more of a roommate than a son. Years ago, as a joke, I had started calling her by her first name, Jessica, instead of "Mom," but she never even noticed. She was short and a bit chubby, had dirty blonde hair and green eyes, always wore business skirts that were too tight for her and she walked in high heel shoes as if she were still learning how. She carried her briefcase and a large purse everywhere she went.

When we got back from the hospital, she heated up some *chiles rellenos* in a Styrofoam container, and we ate at the table. We didn't say much to each other, but she told me that from now on I wasn't going to have any special privileges.

"You mean, I can't use the Mercedes!" I said. "How will I get to the country club?"

"Go to hell, Victor," she said.

"See you there, Jessica," I said.

She held her fork and pointed it at me. "You stay away from that Freddy guy. He's bad news. *¿Me entiendes?* I have eyes everywhere. And they tell me things about you, Victor."

"I thought eyes *see*. If they *tell* you things, they must be mouths. Eyes can't talk."

"Do you know how hard it is to live with you? You always want to make me feel like I'm this small." She put down her fork and showed me with her thumb and finger how small I made her feel, about a quarter of an inch. "*En serio*, I thought I could be a good mother to you. But I'm at the end of my wit."

"You mean your wit's end, *mensa*."

"Don't start with that," she said. She put her head in her hands. Then she took a deep breath and looked up at me. "Don't make fun of me!"

"I was just kidding."

"But that don't do nothing for you, does it? You're still the same. Just like your father."

Here's my father in a nutshell: When I was about four years old, I found this scrawny kitten in a dumpster, and I named her Pepita. I carried her everywhere, and I placed her down on a table, a couch, a closed toilet seat. She would wait for me to carry her to the next spot, as if she hated to have to walk on her own. To me she was like a royal cat too important to have to walk anywhere herself. To everyone else, she looked like a drowned rat, like a street cat. One time Pepita was out in the backyard by herself, and I saw through the window that she was recoiling in pain every few seconds, like she was being bitten by spiders. Then I noticed that right before she flinched, there was a sound from somewhere like a blunt hiss, a BB gun. Someone was shooting at her. She was being barraged by so many BBs that she didn't know where to run. She'd go one way and a BB would spit dirt into her face and she'd run the other way. I realized that there was more than one shooter, and then I saw the men who lived on the other side of the fence shooting at Pepita, laughing. I ran to my father, who was fixing his Monte Carlo in the garage, and I told him. He stood up, a wrench still in his fist, and said, "Let's go."

I remember how it felt walking down the sidewalk behind my father, his fists clenched, how proud I was, because I knew he could kick ass. We got to the house, and he unlatched the gate, pushed it open and went into their backyard like he owned the place. I stayed in the front yard, afraid the men would shoot us, but he was gone for a long time. I wanted to see. I went through the gate, walked past the side of the house, and by the time I got into the backyard, one of the men was sitting on the lawn, looking up at my father like a cholo being questioned on the sidewalk by the police. The other man had his head down like a child ashamed of something he had done, and my father held both BB rifles in one hand, and in the other hand he still had the wrench.

❄ ❄ ❄

My father met Jessica when she worked at a Taco Truck, "Tacos Jessica," owned by her father and named after her. My dad would come every day around 10 a.m., before the lunch rush, because he was courting her. She was old-fashioned and wouldn't just go out with him, so he came back everyday, ordered two *al pastor* tacos and ate them standing up under the window. They would talk about things, all kinds of things he had told me. Although years later Jessica would tell me that all they really talked about was math, that my father was so passionate about it that he would write equations on napkins and explain them to her. She looked down at him, hunched over a piece of paper with a lot of numbers and letters and wonder how someone so "street looking" could love math so much.

He brought her flowers, serenaded her below the window of the taco truck, and after a very long time, she finally agreed to go out with him. Months later they were married. She hardly spoke English, and my father spoke bad, Chicano Spanish, so she started taking Bible classes at a nearby evangelical church just so she could learn the language properly. Unfortunately, the version of the Bible they used was King James, which my mom thought was proper English. For a few years, she would go around saying stuff like, "Thou art late," when my father came home, or "What dost thou desireth for dinner?" She eventually learned proper English, but every now and then some Biblical language would slip out, like she'd yell, *"You idiot! What is wrong with thee?"*

They had three kids, but all of them died at birth or just came out already dead. All three of them were stillborn, Diego, Ezekiel and Sara. My stillborn siblings. That was what they called kids who didn't make it. Stillborn.

Right when they were about to give up trying to have kids, they had me.

And I lived.

They watched me, nervously, but even after a few years, I still lived.

"My Apache! Thou art a miracle," my mom used to say to me.

My father got an associate's degree in math and got a decent job working as a dispatcher for a major food distributor, managing their entire frozen food warehouse. No matter what the season, he wore jackets and gloves to work, as if every day was the cruelest winter. When the company fired him for a reason I will never know about, he started working in an auto body shop with his uncle. That's where he worked until he died.

He died without insurance, without benefits, with nothing more than a hundred dollars in his checking account. My mother's family had gone back to Chihuahua, all but her sister La Malinche, who went up north for many years, somewhere north of Seattle.

My mom either had to move us to Mexico or she had to find a job. She sold my father's house and a got a job at the Taco Palace #3. She was there for years when the owner—some old guy who I always thought was a pervert—asked her to be his manager. Now she worked long hours. She said that she was saving up so I could go to college, but then she started taking classes too. She wanted to get a degree in business management.

Now she wore business skirts and blazers. She always carried a briefcase. She wore high heels, so she didn't seem too short. If you saw her coming down the hallway with a mock leather briefcase, you might think she was a successful business woman. Sometimes she came home still acting all bossy, as if our apartment were the restaurant and she wanted things to run her way.

"From now on," she said, on the night I came home. "I'm going to run a tight slip."

I couldn't help it. "Ship, mensa. The expression is 'tight ship.'"

She stood up, left her dish on the table and went to her room. In spite of how slow I could move in my bandages, I cleaned up the table, washed the dishes, then turned off the lights in the kitchen. I sat at the couch and watched a few episodes of *Weeds*. I had already seen the entire series, but I only liked season one, so I watched it so many times I knew what the characters were going to say next.

I got sleepy. I turned off the TV and got up to go to bed.

I went to Jessica's door and knocked a quick beat. "I'm going to bed, Jess," I said. "Good night."

"Good night, *m'ijo*," she said.

One day, several days after I had gotten out of the hospital, Equis was sitting on the couch watching TV.

I decided to draw him. He had severe acne all over his face and neck, so many clusters of pimples, red and purple and some of them open sores.

I got my gel pens, a sketchpad, and I drew. I made him look as stupid and ugly as possible, his tongue sticking out like an idiot, slobber coming down his chin. I drew his head so big that it filled the page. I made his pimples look like rotting peaches broken open, with flies swarming around the syrupy flesh. As I sketched, he was watching an episode of *Weeds*, one of the later seasons when the main character hooks up with a Mexican drug lord. Equis had a pocketknife, and he opened and closed it as he watched. "Here," I said, pulling the sketch from the pad and throwing it at Equis.

He looked at it. "Aw, that's messed up," he said.

"Let's get out of here," I said. "Let's do something."

"What about the spies?"

"The hell with them. I don't care. Let's go to River Park or something."

"All right. Let's go."

"You better not take the knife," I said. "If you get busted that's evidence for my mom to think we're in a gang."

"We *should* be in a crew," he said.

He pulled out the knife, opened it with only his thumb.

"We'd be the pimpest gangsters, ever!"

"You mean the pimpliest."

"Hey, this is a medical condition!" he said, pointing to his face.

"What is it called, uglyitis?"

As I looked around for bus fare, Equis went into my room, then into the bathroom. When he came out, his face was wet, and his hair had been slicked back with water. "You got any cologne?" he asked.

"I don't wear that stuff."

"You should," he said. "Then maybe girls would like your ugly butt."

He lifted the front of his T-shirt, smelled it and made a face. "I smell like a taco truck."

"You smell like your mom's kitchen," I said, "That's how you always smell."

"*¿En serio?*" he asked, sniffing his shirt, his arms, his underarms. "I smell like a taco truck!"

"Let's go."

He walked out of the door before me, and I turned around, looked at the empty apartment.

We ended up on the far north side of town at Woodward, a huge park near a neighborhood so rich they had tall, stone walls and entrances into their streets, with the names of the development company written in fancy rock letters—names like the Renaissance Estates or Sherwood Meadows, places like Agrestic in *Weeds*. We entered the park, which was supposed to be open to anyone, even poor people, and we walked onto the grass and into the tall trees. The park was nice. There were no parks in our neighborhood, and if there were schoolyards, the gates were locked shut with chains. Here it felt like we weren't even in the city. It stretched on and on with lakes and ducks and Japanese gardens. I felt good, relaxed.

"There's more girls at River Park," Equis said.

"Just shut up," I said, walking across a small hill of grass scattered with yellow flowers. I could feel the sun on my face.

We reached a part of the lawn where there was a stream of running water, and there was a grassy knoll that overlooked an expanse of lawn, which reached on until you could see a line of pine trees. We sat down. I sighed, as if I was glad to have arrived there. It was almost quiet. Some little kids were playing in the stream, wading in the water, their pants rolled up to their calves, looking for pretty rocks. Their pregnant mother was sitting on the grass watching them and laughing at their antics.

We were in the shade of a giant tree. I could feel a breeze on my face, and I could hear the wind in the upper branches. Equis was sitting legs crossed, watching the kids, laughing like he wanted to go into the water and play with them.

I closed my eyes. Inside my head I saw a swirl of orange dark and light colors.

"Look," Equis said.

I opened my eyes, and he pointed to something with his chin. I looked across the expanse of lawn sprinkled with tiny yellow flowers and far away I could see someone walking alone.

"A pretty girl," he said.

He didn't say it lustfully, like *Damn, she's fine!* or *I want to get with her!* but like a quiet fact. She was so far away that all we could see were white pants and a red blouse, a red ribbon in her long black hair. She was too far away for us to see her face or any detail—nothing but those strokes of white and red and black across the green of the park. It was true though, she was a pretty girl. We watched her slide across the field until she became a white dot on the horizon.

Later, I would wonder why we both thought she was beautiful. She was too far away to see, but in our minds we saw a pretty girl, a judgment based on the most minimal of color and shape, those slashes of white and red and black. Later on, a few years into the future, I would see a lot of Van Gogh paintings up close. I would see how he could create—with a few strokes—a woman bending over working in the fields, a peasant boy and girl sleeping in the hay, a waiter standing in a cafe doorway, and I'd think of that pretty girl in Woodward Park.

But back to the sad story of Victor Reyes: I thought of something.

"Oh, shit! What day is it?" I asked Equis.

He was standing up in the stream to his ankles, his shoes and socks on a rock. He was looking for stones. He was examining one he had taken from the stream. "You know what, eh? This looks like a moon rock, *en serio.*" He turned it over in his fingers to look at all sides. Then he held it up to the sun.

"What day is it?" I asked again.

"Tuesday," he said.

"I thought it was Wednesday! My mom only works half a day today. Where's your knife?"

"At your place," he said. "You told me not to bring it."

"Where did you leave it?"

"I don't 'member. In your room, I guess."

"Where in my room?"

"I don't know."

"Did you hide it?"

He thought about it for a while, like he was doing a complex math problem in his head. Then the answer came to him. He snapped his fingers. "It's on the bed."

꒳ ꒳ ꒳

When I walked into the apartment, she was sitting at the kitchen table. In front of her was the knife. I sat across from her. I said, "It's not mine. I promise you."

She pulled her purse toward her, and she put an arm inside of it and felt around. She took out her wallet. She unsnapped the top, pulled out some paper money and put it on the table. Then she went into another small compartment, pulled out coins and let those drop on the table too. Her fingers were chubby, almost white, and as she unrolled some single dollar bills, her fingers seemed to be jittering with controlled rage. She stacked dollars with dollars, fives with fives, quarters with quarters, nickels with nickels, dimes with dimes, slowly, deliberately, like an old-fashioned bank teller who had all the time in the world. When she was done stacking and counting, she pulled back her hands and held them on the table in front of her.

"Do you know what that is?"

"Money, if I'm not mistaken. *Se llama feria.*"

"Don't say *feria* to mean money," she commanded. "I won't have any cholo talk in my house. If you want to speak Spanish, *no es feria, es dinero. Es en efectivo. ¿Me entiendes?*"

"What's in a name?" I said.

"You want to guess how much it is?"

"Is there a prize?"

"It's just enough for a Greyhound bus ticket to Modesto. One way."

"Are you leaving town?"

"I'm not," she said. "You are. I'm sending you to spend the rest of the summer with your tía."

"La Malinche?"

"Pack your bags."

"But she's crazy."

"Pack your bags now!"

"Don't send me there, please."

"She's tougher than me. She used to fight forest fires. Maybe she can help you be decent. I thought I could help you."

"I don't want to go to Tía Malinche."

"But you don't want to be a good son neither."

"I'm not a thug. I don't even like to fight. I swear."

"Don't swear. *Let your yea be yea and your nay be nay. Anything else commeth from evil.*" She held her fists in front of her and made a sound of frustration, as if she wanted to box me, or as if the rage was concentrated into tiny hotspots in the middle of her fists. She hammered the table with both fists and stood up, not like she was going anywhere, but as if she had to convert some of her anger into motion.

She crossed the kitchen and stood at the window, in front of the sink, her back to me. She was wearing a business skirt and a silky blouse. She was looking out the window. Her body was trying to relax, but there was so much tension in her that you could see her legs twitching, as if she were tensing her calf muscles. Her elbow, the one resting on the counter, trembled slightly. She was trying to be at peace, trying to be like a woman in a painting looking out a window at the sea and the boats, but she was full of rage. You could see her neck trembling, even her hair, her ponytail, how it vibrated.

"I got a class," she said. "By the time I get back, you be ready to go."

"It's not my knife," I said.

"Then why do you have it?"

"It belongs to stupid Equis."

"Harold? He's a nice kid. I think you corrupt him."

"Me?"

"You're going to spend the summer with Malinche."

"But she's weird. Wasn't she disowned by your family for being so . . .weird?"

"My father disowns everybody."

"So it runs in the family? You're going to disown me? I thought we were better people than that."

"I'm not disowning you. Not yet. You're staying with Tía Che for the summer."

"Who the hell is Che?"

"Malinche! That's all there is to it. Johnny will be there, your cousin. Do you know he's a student at Berkeley in the college there? Do you know how hard it is to get into that school? You have to be the best student, the top of your class, but that's where he studies. Maybe some smartness will rub off on you."

"Johnny's a dork."

"Ya decidí. Vas con tu tía."

"The entire summer?"

She grabbed her briefcase from the table, went into the other room. "I'll be back after class. You better be here. And you better be sober."

"Sober? When am I not sober?"

"You think I'm a naïve and stupid woman?"

When she left, I stood there not sure what to do.

I had to find a way to convince her to let me stay. My cousin Johnny was a cruel nerd. He used to try and make me cry by twisting the skin of my arm into what he called an Indian sunburn, but I was stubborn and no matter how hard it hurt I fought the tears. I hadn't seen him in many years.

I paced the apartment, back and forth, until an idea hit me.

I'd cook dinner for her!

On Tuesdays, when she got home from class at night, she sluggishly cooked something for herself. Tonight, I would have dinner waiting, and she would be so stuffed and satisfied that she would want me to stay.

I looked in the refrigerator. We had a twelve-pack of Diet Pepsi, an open package of corn tortillas, some lunch-

meats and a plate with a half slab of Spam. There was a
bottle of grape Snapple and jars of mustard and *salsa
verde* and pickles and green olives. There were also milk
and eggs and cheese and some loose jalapeños. There
were leftover *chiles rellenos* from her work, in a Styrofoam
to-go container. In the bottom drawer we had lettuce and
tomatoes. I looked in the freezer and saw frozen ground
beef and a baggie of frozen chicken breasts. I pulled out
the ground beef.

I had all the ingredients for tacos, but then I thought
of something.

She worked all day at the Taco Palace #3, so the last
thing she would want for dinner would be tacos.

I decided I would Google some recipes.

We had a computer that we shared. It was on a desk
in her bedroom. I went in there, started it up and waited.
Her room had clothes all over the bed and furniture. It
was the messiest room in the house, because no one was
around to clean it up. It smelled like perfume. She wore
a lot of it, so it was in all of her clothes, her bed sheets,
the curtains that were always shut. The computer was
kind of slow.

I went online to look for a recipe, something exotic,
something special that would convince her to let me stay
with her. Most of the recipes required ingredients we
didn't have, but there was a small grocery store down the
street, and I could gather up enough change to buy what
I needed. But what? Something she never had before.
Something she would love. Something a gang banger
would never make for his mother in a million years.

I decided on Pasta a la Norma. I would change the
name and tell her it was called *Pasta a la Jessica*. I found
it on recipe.com. I printed it out on my mom's inkjet

printer that shook the table when it printed. I went to my bedroom to get the cash box, which I hid on the top of the closet. It was a metal box with a little key. I opened it and took out a five. It was my stash money.

My room was clean, organized, and against the open window—looking out onto the apartment parking lot— stood my little desk with sketchpads and pens and charcoals lined up in perfect rows. There was also a picture in a frame of my father in the auto body shop, holding up his arms to the camera, a beer bottle in one of his hands. It always struck me how dark he was in that picture. You could see the white of his eyes and his white teeth like in a negative, because whoever snapped it didn't use a flash. The shop in the background was dark, and all you could see was a car with Bondo all over it. Everything else was in shadows, shaded figures surrounding my father.

We already had onions and garlic, but I needed everything else. It called for olive oil, but we only had vegetable oil. I wasn't sure how much of a difference that would make, but I wanted it to be perfect, to follow the recipe to the letter. Then I noticed the Modesto money was still on the table, paper bills and stacks of coins. It was an investment in my future, I figured, and she would be so happy that she would forgive me for using some of it. I grabbed a handful of cash and shoved it into my pocket

I left the apartment like a thief. It was a hot afternoon. The neighbor lady was sitting in a chair outside her door playing Mario Brothers on her handheld player, one of those old ones from back in her days.

On the second floor where we lived, there were no balconies, just a wrap-around cement sidewalk railed by black iron bars, a path past our front doors. Meche was sitting right outside her door. Her front door was open and you could hear Oldies music coming from inside. It sounded like *Al Green's Greatest Hits*, one of my father's favorite albums.

I liked Death Metal so sometimes when I heard an Oldies song that Chicanos like my father used to love, I couldn't help but imagine a Death Metal version. Something as Motown as "Midnight Train to Georgia" would be sung with monster-like vocals, a demonic scream.

He's leaving! He's leaving!

Now I imagined Al Green as a Death Metal act, with that monstrous scream.

I'm so tired of being alone!!!!

So tired of being alone!!!

And the guitar would be loud and distorted like a metal scream.

Why don't you help me girl!!!!?????.

Meche was playing her game. It was kind of funny to see, because you didn't expect someone so old to like video games, especially on such a small screen. She didn't even have good eyes, but I guess anyone could get hooked on that stuff. There was a time when Equis and I would spend all day playing video games, but we could never afford the more advanced systems, so we got bored with the ancient graphics. My mom's computer was too old to play games online—everything always froze and you had to restart the computer, which took about an hour.

I walked backwards and went around the other way to the stairs. When I was street-level, I felt safe.

I felt pretty good walking along the street going to the store to get food for my mother. I felt like I was a character in some movie about a nice neighborhood, maybe a musical like a Disney cartoon.

I could see myself busting out in song and dance, and all the little street kids playing and running around half naked singing along with me.

I'm going to the store!
And the little kids sing:
He's going to the store!
And the people at the bus stop sing:
He's going to the store!
Then me:
To buy some food for my mother!
Then them:
Food for his mother!
Then me: *What kind of thug buys food for his mother?*
All: *Food for his mother!*

✻ ✻ ✻

I walked into the Sánchez Market. The place was smaller than a big grocery store, but bigger than a mini-mart, and it smelled good too, because they sold fresh tacos and burritos. Way in the back they had a butcher who could cut your pieces of meat, and they sold *chicharrones* and *chorizo* by the weight. I loved the smell of Mexican stores. They were different, because when you walked into a big North American grocery store, there were no smells, there was just white light and bright colors. Mexican stores smelled like real food.

"Hey, there he is!" said Mr. Sánchez, pointing at me.

He was standing by the register ringing up some lady's stuff, about a thousand cans of evaporated milk.

Maybe she was one of those cat ladies and had them all over her house.

"Hey, Mr. Sánchez," I said.

"There he is!" he said again.

That was all Mr. Sánchez ever said to me, *There he is!* The old lady looked at me too.

"Afternoon, ma'am," I said like a character in a musical.

She nodded her head and said, *"Dios te bendiga."*

Call me superstitious, but I liked being blessed by an elder.

I grabbed one of those baskets you carry around when you don't need enough stuff for a shopping cart.

The first thing I looked for was eggplant, but I wasn't sure what it was. My mom and I ate pretty basic stuff, and I cooked eggs, tacos, bowls of cereal with toast. I went to the egg section and looked at all the cartons of eggs, because I thought I might find eggplant there. The recipe said you were supposed to slice it, so I knew it couldn't be a regular egg. I pictured a slab of cake or something that was made from egg whites, but I couldn't find anything that said eggplant. I looked down the aisle and saw that Mr. Sánchez was alone for a second, so I went down the aisle to ask him. He got bigger and bigger the closer I got, and he saw me coming. "There he is!" he said.

"Mr. Sánchez, do you have eggplant?"

"¿Qué es?"

"Uh, *No sé. Se llama* eggplant."

"Eck Plent?"

Then it occurred to me that maybe he always said that (*There he is!*), because he didn't know much more English than that.

I showed him the recipe.

"Pasta a la Norma?" he asked.

"*Sí, se llama* eggplant. *Pero ¿qué es?*"

He put on his glasses and examined the recipe as if it were a secret code.

"Marta," he said, to the cashier on the next register. "*¿Qué es* eggplant?"

Marta was a chubby woman in her 30s. You know she had a crazy past because she had tattoos on her hands, like a *chola*, but now she was trying to do something with her life and probably had a couple of kids. She didn't take her fingers or her eyes from the register as she totaled some stuff. "*Berenjena,*" she said.

"*Ah,* ekk plan. *Por supuesto. Ven.*"

He led me down an aisle, past dairy products and sodas. I got this weird sensation that Mr. Sánchez was going to take me to the back of the store, through some secret door into a dark room where eggs grew on vines and you had to chop them off with machetes.

But when we got to the vegetables, he stopped. He grabbed this purple thing shaped like a melting clock. "*Aquí está,*" he said.

"Are you sure that's it?" I asked.

He pulled his iPhone out of his apron pocket and said the letters as he entered them, "B. E. R. E . . . "

Then he pressed enter.

"*Mira,*" he said. And he showed me the screen. *Eggplant,* it said.

"Well, thanks," I said.

"*¿Qué vas a hacer?*" he asked,

"I'm cooking dinner for my mother," I said.

"Ah, see? You're nice kid."

That made me feel good, because if a stranger could think I was a nice kid, surely my mom would think the same thing. Next I had to find linguini, which I knew was some sort of pasta. I went to the spaghetti section. They had spaghetti, lasagna, rice, but no linguini. I looked over at Mr. Sánchez, but he was at the register. I didn't want to bother him again. I saw a man with a basket shopping for some food, and I went over to him and asked if he knew what linguini was.

"It's pasta," he said, "like spaghetti."

"They probably don't have it here, huh?"

He put down the can of tomato sauce he was holding and went over to the pasta section. He looked around but couldn't find linguini. "I would just use spaghetti," he said. "Same thing."

"Thanks," I said and pulled a box of spaghetti from the shelf and put it in my basket.

Next, I needed olive oil.

I found it pretty easily, but it was like ten dollars a bottle, so I figured the sign must have been wrong. I grabbed a bottle and examined it. It was called Borges. Extra Virgin.

I walked around the store looking for an employee. I saw Marta walking to the back of the store, undoing her apron, maybe going on break. She had thick arms and big fists, like she could kick ass if she wanted to. I asked her if she knew how much the Borges was.

"$8.99," she said. "Just use vegetable oil. That's helluva lot cheaper."

"That'll work the same?" I asked.

"Same damn stuff," she said.

"All right!" I said. "I got some at home."

I put the Borges back on the shelf and went to get the Romano cheese. I wasn't sure what that was, but in the cheese section there was only Mexican cheese (*queso seco*), American cheese (individually wrapped slices), Monterey Jack and Cheddar. I picked up the Kraft American cheese and I thought of my father. It was weird too, the way I thought of him. I didn't picture him or remember what he looked like. As I reached for the individually wrapped slices of cheese, I felt him also reaching for them. It was a strange sensation, like cold shivers, and I shook it off and remembered my Broadway musical.

I sang.

I'm looking for cheese.

And all the store employees and customers would look over and sing:

He's looking for cheese.

To cook some food for my mother!

And Mr. Sánchez would sing solo:

Cheese for his motheeeeeeeer!

I saw a big box of Velveeta. It was a lot of cheese for less money. I was certain it would be as good as Romano. I put it in my basket and went to pay.

On the way home I walked down the street with my plastic grocery bags, one hanging in each hand, and I could see my shadow and the shadow of the bags walking next to me and sliding by slowly on a tall wooden fence. My shadow looked like an old man walking home by himself.

There were a lot of people out, a lot of traffic, because it was barely after 5:00 p.m. and everyone was coming home from work. I passed by a homeless man who asked me for money, so I gave him 50 cents, which was the minimal you could offer. If you gave them pennies and nickels, it was probably like an insult. You had to give them at least a quarter, but 50 cents was the normal amount.

At an intersection I saw a red Hummer at the stoplight, and my heart jumped out of my chest. I thought I was dying. I stood frozen.

For the first time, I remembered details about how I got killed.

Some guy had pulled a sawed-off rifle from his flannel shirt and put it at my stomach. His face was in a grimace, as if he hated me more than anything in the world. He yelled something to me.

Who was he? Why did he hate me? Why couldn't I remember anything else? All this time I had been content not to remember anything. Equis didn't know, Freddy didn't know. Jessica was the only one who thought she knew what happened, but her version was like a scene from a 1980s movie about Chicano gangs. I was content to not know any of the details of being shot and being legally dead for 2.2 minutes. But now, something slipped into my memory, some fleeting image, and I was afraid the door would remain open and memories would come out one by one like ghosts from a closet.

I could hardly breathe, and I was getting dizzy. People at the bus stop looked at me like they were worried for me.

⚘ ⚘ ⚘

There was a big difference between Romano and Velveeta cheese. First of all, one of them is Italian, white and *enhances* the flavor of foods. The other cheese was a florescent orange, and it beat the crap out of every taste it encountered. It came in a cardboard box, and you couldn't grate it—which the recipe called for—because it was too soft and squeezed against the cheese grater and turned gooey on your fingers.

I looked at the picture of Pasta a la Norma on the internet, and it looked nothing like what I was about to create. I thought I could get the Velveeta to at least look like Romano cheese, so I put the entire orange brick in a sauce pan and added milk. I cooked it. I figured I could freeze it, and when it turned solid, I could crumble it over the pasta like the recipe called for. On the flame, it turned to liquid pretty quickly, but when I looked at the clock, I realized I only had about twenty minutes left before my mom would get home. I was about to give up.

That was when my little friend came to visit.

I used to have imaginary friends, because being an only child I often had to entertain myself. I imagined an entire community of friends, people, angels, giant rabbits and although I hadn't done this in years, *Poof!* a new friend appeared in the kitchen.

He was an Italian chef, a fat man with a big moustache and curly hair under a tall, white chef's hat. He was a cartoon. *"Bonjourno!"* he said.

"'Zup dog?" I said.

"What is this *dog?*" he asked. He had a fake and exaggerated Italian accent.

"Can you help me?" I asked. "My mom will be home soon and I don't have any idea what to do with all this stuff."

"Okay, I'm going to a-help you, yes? But I a-have to hurry and get back, because Meche she needs me. I am the little man in her video game."

"You're not Mario! You're that chef on the cartoon about the rat!"

"No. I am a one hundred percent Italiano! Now, you must remember dis: Cookin,' she is an art. You must treat the process like you do when you draw a picture. You're an artist, yes?"

"Well, sometimes I draw."

"When you cook-a, be creative. Imagine your dinner into being."

"Creative, huh?"

"Yes, and remember, what matters to you the most-a is the process, yes? The act of drawing. You must-a love the process or the product is-a very bad, yes?"

"Yeah, that's true," I said.

And then it hit me.

I saw the finished meal in my head. It wasn't Pasta a la Norma. It was something new, something I created. It was a new kind of spaghetti with a Velveeta Cheese sauce and jalapeños. I remembered we had some fresh ones in the refrigerator, so I pulled them out and sliced them very thinly.

"That's a-more a-like it," said my trite friend.

"Thanks, Mario."

I put a little oil in a pan, because I was going to brown the jalapeños before I added them to the cheese sauce, but Mario said, "What are you doing?"

"What?" I asked.

"First put some garlic."

Before I put in the jalapeños, I sautéed a little garlic. The smell filled the apartment, and it was good. It smelled like a fancy restaurant. Next, I put some onions that I had sliced and pushed them around the pan with a wooden spoon. I liked the way they sizzled and released their smell. Only after they were cooked did I put in the jalapeños. Now I was having fun, I even started singing and my imaginary friend sang too.

Mama mia

Pizzaria

Flavor of Italy!

Then it occurred to me that I was making Mexican spaghetti, Chicano spaghetti I could call it, and suddenly my Italian friend turned into a Mexican.

He wore a big, Mexican sombrero.

He put his face over the pan and took in the smells. "*¡Ay Dios mío!*" he said. "*¡Qué delicioso!*"

After I sautéed the onions, garlic and jalapeños, I added them to the cheese sauce that was still simmering on the stove. I stuck in the wooden spoon, and pulled it out and tasted the sauce.

It was good, but still, something was missing.

Then I remembered the frozen chicken breasts in the freezer. I took them out and put them in the microwave to defrost. When they were done, I sliced them into tiny pieces. I put on a frying pan, added a bit of oil and then some garlic. As that sizzled, I salt-and-peppered the chicken pieces. Then I put them into the pan. I loved the way the chicken sizzled. "The chicken might be a little bland," Mario said. I remembered the spice rack someone had once gotten my mom for Christmas which she never used. I pulled it out of the cupboard and started pulling off the tops of the tiny jars and smelling them. I wanted good spices. I loved the names of them: cinnamon, basil, mustard seed, saffron, cloves, nutmeg and tamarind. I smelled each one, trying to find the accent that I thought would go well with the Chicano Spaghetti. Then I found it, the smell seemed like a perfect match. It was called cumin. I sprinkled just a tiny bit onto the chicken. Then I pinched an even smaller amount of basil, so small no one would even notice, kind of like when I would shade someone's eyes in a drawing. The technique was subtle, but it added a depth to the drawing, even if the viewer didn't notice it.

I took the chicken and added it to the cheese sauce. I stirred it all with a wooden spoon and I tasted it. The chicken was good, but the sauce still had some missing element that had more to do with texture than taste. It was runny, a little too watery. What was missing?

Then I remembered the eggplant. I had forgotten all about it. I took it out of the bag and wasn't sure what to do with it.

"Hmm, that's a problem," said Mario, who was Italian again. He looked at the big purple ball in my hand. "You must-a cut her."

I sliced it into slabs about a half inch thick. I was quick, because time was running out. "Don't make dirty your shirt," said Mario. I put on an apron. The slices seemed kind of meaty, like steaks. I thought maybe I could cook them in oil and garlic and serve them on the side of the Chicano Spaghetti.

We didn't have a lot of pans, so I was about to dump the juice from the chicken into the sink, but then I got a better idea. All the broth from the chicken might be exactly what the sauce needed. So I spooned it into the cheese sauce, a little at a time, stirring it, tasting and adding more. I ended up putting in all the broth. It was perfect.

I pulled eggs out of the refrigerator, broke them, put them into a bowl and stirred like I was making an omelet. My father used to make a good omelet. He loved to cook, but it was like I was remembering it for the first time. He stood at the stove, and I handed him some slices of American cheese.

I added basil and a little caraway seed. I poured the eggs onto a plate, and then I dipped the slices of eggplant into the solution. I fried them.

I looked at the clock and saw that she would be home any second. The food was done. I quickly set the table, washed the dishes and I waited for her.

I told her that the dish was made special for her, and that I called it Spaghetti Jessica. She put her hands over her mouth. "*Mi apache,*" she said.

I told her I wanted her to feel special, because she worked so hard and had so much to put up with because of me. I told her I was sorry. I told her I used a little bit of the bus money, and her only reaction was to laugh.

And it was a great meal, except for the eggplant, which was soggy with raw egg. We even talked. She told me about the Taco Palace #3. There was no Taco Place #1 or #2 but when the owner opened the restaurant, he had big plans to open up a chain of them. Now he was getting old and wanted her to take over. His daughters, who didn't know anything about the business and who had never cared about it, suddenly wanted to run things. They thought the old man was going to die any day, and they were making it hard for my mom, treating her as if she was trying to inherit the business.

I told Jessica that she should buy the restaurant and run it herself, call it Tacos Jessica. After dinner, she rose to wash the dishes, but I told her that she should go study. I'd clean up.

☙ ☙ ☙

Later that night, when she was in her room studying, I sat at the couch with my pens and sketchpad. I was drawing Mario, the imaginary Italian chef. I did him cartoon style.

I put him standing in a kitchen before boiling pots.

I drew a live chicken in his hand, and he was lowering it into a pot. The chicken looked nervous. It was an okay drawing, I guess. I mean, not as good as Lalo, but I was mostly doing it for fun. I shaded the background so that the kitchen looked a bit dark, and I put tiny shapes—a few dashes of the pen—that looked like people watching Mario in the kitchen. I drew small discs in their hands so it looked like they had their empty plates ready for food. I gave them dot eyes and smiles, and on some of them I crowned their heads with long curves flowing down to indicate the hair of women. I drew about ten people that way, the most minimal detail, but somehow, they had personalities, like the pretty girl in the park.

I felt someone behind me.

"That's pretty good," she said.

"Thanks," I said.

"You have talent," she said.

I put down the pad, because it was weird for me to draw while someone was looking over my shoulder. She just stood there, looking down at me.

"I saw the Pasta a la Norma on the internet," she said.

"You searched my history," I said.

"Of course," she said.

"I tried that recipe," I said. "But I couldn't get all the stuff it required, so I just improvised, I guess."

"Thank you," she said. "That you were able to make something up . . . and it was so good. I'm taking the leftovers for lunch tomorrow—that you were able to do that, *m'ijo*, it's a good sign that you're creative and intelligent."

She sat down next to me on the couch and put her hand on my cheek.

"You're not a bad boy, are you?" she asked.

"I'm not in a gang."

"I'm sorry," she said, and she took me in her arms and held me. She had on a lot of perfume.

"You don't have to go to Modesto," she said. "You're a good boy. But don't even let me see you and a knife in the same room, okay? Unless it's for chopping onions." She kissed me on the head and held me tight. I wanted to push her away because I couldn't breathe with all that perfume, but I didn't do anything. I just let her hold me until her arms got tired.

⁂ ⁂ ⁂

All there was to do all summer was sit around the apartment, draw and read books. I couldn't watch TV anymore, because after finding the knife she unhooked it, said she had read a study that shows TV can make kids violent.

So I read the books on her shelf, mostly what she had from her City College classes. I found a thin novel called *Death in Venice*, which was about some old guy who goes on vacation to die. I drew a picture of him standing on a boat about ready to take off for Venice.

I found a poet named Lorca, a collection of bilingual poems, Spanish on one side, English on the other. Although my Spanish wasn't great, I could read them in both languages.

I loved Lorca's images, especially the ones that didn't make sense.

He had this one poem that started with, *"Verde que te quiero verde.* Green it's that I love you green."

I had no idea what it meant, but it inspired me to draw green people, all kinds of green people, normal people in the city, only green.

Verde que te quiero verde.

Lorca wrote a lot about death. I was curious about death and dying, I guess because I had experienced it. I looked up "life after death" on the internet and found the term *Ars Moriendi*, the Art of Dying. There were a bunch of books about how to die.

Our two-bedroom apartment was small, but I started to pace from room to room thinking, *How is dying an art?*

One time I turned on some Death Metal and drew a bunch of faces, filling pages and pages of faces piled on top of each other, most of them looking as if they were suffering, like they were burning in hell. They were faces of the dead.

When the temperatures reached the 100s and the swamp cooler barely did anything to cool down the apartment, I would walk from room to room to room like a zombie or a philosopher (which was the same thing), and I tried to think hard about life. I pretended like I was grappling with big issues, but I was making fun of philosophers. "Maybe the meaning of life is to prepare for death," I said aloud one afternoon. "Yes, yes! That's it! Preparing for death is the Art of Dying. It's the meaning of life!"

Poof!

"That's a-crazy talk," said Mario, appearing in the kitchen. He removed the lid from a pot on the stovetop, looked in and made a face. "Let's cook something!"

After that day, I cooked a lot. I put two fans in the small kitchen and made lunch for me and dinner almost every night for Jessica. In the evenings, when she was home, she would give me grocery money, and I would walk to Sánchez Market to get the food we needed for the next few days. I got pretty good at meatloaf, which I served with mashed potatoes and corn and biscuits right out of the oven. One afternoon I tried fish tacos, Baja style, the way Equis' mom made them.

Equis seemed to like them. He was sitting in the living room on the couch, leaning over the coffee table where he had the plate of fish tacos, eating them like french fries.

"*Mama mia!*" Mario said. "That boy can eat!"

He cleared off his plate and asked me if there were any left, but I told him the remainder of the fish was for my mom. I would cook them fresh for her that night. He lifted the plate and licked everything off, then he sat back on the couch and burped.

"They're pretty good, huh?"

"They were shit compared to the way my momers makes them."

"You ate a bunch of them, fool."

"I got to admit. You're getting pretty good at being like a girl. You'll make a good housewife someday."

"You're lucky I don't slap you down," I said.

"Damn!" he said, dividing the word into two syllables, as if I were no threat at all.

I walked over to the couch and stood before him, looking down at him. He crossed his arms.

"Come on," I said. "Get up. Let's go at it." I got into a boxer's stance and slap-boxed the air, *one-two-three*, two times fast, my fingers coming a few inches from his face.

"Leave me alone, fool."

"Come on, let's go," I said, and I grabbed him like a rag doll and pulled him to his feet, but he just stood there like a teenager, and he didn't lift his arms for a slap fight.

"Come on, boy," I said, *one-two-three*, and on the last jab, my fingertips grazed his face.

"Stop that, man," he said. "I ain't wasting my time with you."

"Quit saying 'ain't,' *pendejo*!"

"Just leave me alone, all right, Victor."

"Ah, you know I'm just playing with you, bro."

"Well it gets old pretty fast," he said. "I'm serious too."

"All right, I'm sorry. I'll make it up to you. What do you want me to cook tomorrow?"

"How about enchiladas?"

"Too easy. Give me something more challenging."

"I don't know. Something fancy, like chicken breast or something, like with that stuff they put all over it, you know, mushrooms and sauce."

"How about beef stroganoff?"

"I don't even know what that is."

"I've been wanting to try it," I said.

The next day I did make beef stroganoff, spending most of the morning preparing it, chopping, slicing and measuring. Even though it wasn't a dish from Italy, I sang aloud with Mario what sounded to me like Italian songs, the only two I knew. *Mama mia, pizzeria!* And *Volare! Oooh Oooh Oooh.*

I sang, set the table and waited for Equis.

When Equis and I were little kids, we lived across the street from each other. I remember the day I met him. I was outside playing in the alley when I saw him sitting behind a garbage dumpster, a glass bubble on his head with NASA written across the top. He had a line of beer bottles in front of him, his controls, and for a steering wheel (because he must have thought astronauts steer their way to the moon), he used a paper plate with a brown chicken *mole* stain in the center like a soiled diaper. He made puttering sounds with his lips pressed together and saliva shooting out. When he saw me standing there, he said, "Wanna go to space?" and we became instant friends.

For years, Jessica treated him like a son, because more than anyone I had ever known, Equis' mission in life, other than to be the world's youngest astronaut, was to please adults. He was obedient. He did all that he was told with an intense concentration. He was determined to be the world's youngest astronaut, and he always wore that glass bubble, taking it off only to eat and sleep or when his mother told him to take it off. He got excellent marks in school, always the teacher's pet, the kind of kid who cleans blackboard erasers after class, slapping himself into a cloud of white dust as the teacher bends over her desk grading papers.

It seemed that Equis was marked for a successful life, but as the subjects in school became more demanding and required more mental energy than simple subjection to authority, he couldn't keep up. By junior high he was flunking most of his classes. He just couldn't grasp the math problems, couldn't get a handle on grammar and spelling.

When we were teenagers, he still had his space helmet, but only as a decoration, sitting on his chest of drawers. He still had posters of NASA space missions on his wall. One time I was going to sneak up to his window, because I had some pot and wanted to get high. I looked into his room and saw him sitting on the bed wearing his glass bubble.

I never said anything to him about it. I turned away, got stoned by myself.

When I was shot by those thugs, I spent ten days in the hospital. He was there with me every day, all day long, from eight to eight, acting as if we were just hanging out.

✺ ✺ ✺

When he hadn't shown up by one, I sat by myself at the table and ate.

It was good, but I was a little pissed off that he hadn't called. So when he did show up after 3 p.m., I let him have it. I told him how inconsiderate it was, because he knew I was going to cook beef stroganoff.

"I'm sorry, bro. Dang. Why you acting like a mother?"

"You've been drinking too, huh?"

I could smell beer on his breath.

"Sit down," I said. I heated up a plate and put it in front of him.

"What do you want to drink?" I asked him.

I watched him take a first bite, and then a second and then a third, and then he kept shoveling the food in his mouth faster and faster. "This shit is good!"

"You like it?"

"What's on the menu tomorrow?"

One afternoon, after we ate the meatballs and spaghetti I had made, I got my sketchpad and pens. I sat on a chair in the living room, across the couch from where Equis sat. I started to draw him.

"Seriously, bro. I got to admit, you're getting good at cooking shit. If I were you, I'd quit drawing and just cook all the time. You're better at it."

"I just draw for fun," I said.

"Yeah, it's a good thing too. Hey, let's go somewhere," he said, standing up.

"You know I can't."

"Then let's do a beer run."

"My mom would smell it on my breath."

"We'll get some *chicle*, too. Come on!"

"Just chill."

"Chill my ass," he said. He looked around the apartment, as if it were the most uninteresting place in the world, and said, "Can we at least get high?"

I brought out the pipe and we smoked. Then I opened all the windows and sprayed the place with toilet air freshener. Now I was ready to draw.

But Equis got energetic and wanted to go out and do something. He started pacing the apartment, back and forth with so much energy I thought he might walk through a wall. "I gotta get out o' here," he said.

"What are you thinking about?" I asked him.

"Getting out of this place."

"What do you think you're missing that's out there?" I asked, drawing him.

"Stuff. Girls. Parties. Girls. The streets. Cars. The flea market. I don't care. Let's go to the Cherry Auction."

I drew him pacing the living room. I wanted it to be obvious that he was bored and full of energy, not only by his facial expression, but his body, his fists almost clenched, his legs in motion as if he wanted to go even though he had nowhere to go. Over his head I put a cartoon bubble, the thinking bubble, and inside I drew a vague outline of a car and a girl. The sketch wasn't good, nothing like I wanted it to be. When I showed it to Equis, he wasn't even sure what it was. "A ghost in a haunted house?" he said, examining it.

"It's you."

"Don't quit your day job, bro. Come on, let's go!"

After a while, he didn't come around as much anymore, just occasionally to watch a TV show, get high, eat whatever I made that day and then he'd leave. Then he quit coming by at all. I was alone all day, even at night when my mom was in class or in her bedroom studying. I missed Equis. I felt I would go insane if I didn't talk to anyone. I paced the apartment back and forth, talking to myself or listening to Death.

One afternoon, I got a call from Freddy, the man my mom forbade me to see.

At first I didn't recognize the voice.

"Is this the residence of Chi Chi La Rue?" he asked.

"What?"

"Chi Chi," he said. "I'm looking for Chi Chi."

"Chi Chi? She's not here. She's dead. I guess no one told you."

"Get ready," he said. "I'm coming to pick you up."

"You can't. I'm not allowed to hang out with known gang members."

"I'll honk when I get there," he said.

And he hung up.

I was going to call him back and tell him some excuse why I couldn't go. I wouldn't say that my mom wouldn't let me, because that sounded pretty lame. I didn't want him to think I was a little kid. I'd say I was sick or something. Before I even got the chance to hit the talk button on the phone, I heard honking right outside. He honked again and again. I stood there wondering what to do. Then he honked some more, over and over. I was afraid he'd get Meche's attention. If she looked down from the railing and saw him, he wasn't hard to describe.

He was big, she'd tell Jessica. *I mean huge.*

I had no choice but to rush out of the house and tell him to quit honking.

🐾 🐾 🐾

I opened the door and stepped into the heat and the sunlight. It was hot, a dry summer heat, and I saw Freddy sitting in his Chevy Impala. The tunes were loud, a sexy-sounding lady singing about love and sex. I could hear him singing along with her, a high-pitched whine, *Baby, I want you so bad.*

He honked again, this time in little beats as if to go with the music, followed by a long one, and he wailed a high note along with the woman singer . . . *waaaaaaaaaaant so baaaaaad!*

"Shut the hell up," I said.

I got in the car, and the music was too loud to talk to him. "Turn that down!" I yelled.

Freddy was big, seeming even bigger when I was sitting next to him in his car. He was swaying in his seat, as if he were dancing. He smelled as if he had used a full bottle of patchouli oil.

"Turn that down," I yelled again, wanting to plug my nose.

"What?" he yelled.

I reached for his stereo and turned down the volume.

"Do you know how trite you're being?" I asked him.

"Tripe? Isn't that what they put in *menudo*?"

"Trite," I said. "It means stereotypical. You're acting like a stereotype. And you're going to get me busted."

"Busted?" He looked out the window, as if trying to find the undercover cops. "What the hell you do?"

"It's . . . It's stupid. I'm not allowed to leave the apartment."

"Why?"

"I'm a prisoner," I said.

"Call Child Protective Services. Your mom can get arrested for that shit."

Freddy drove me down a busy boulevard.

"Where are we going?" I asked.

"Pa' viejo."

When he was younger, he had lived across the street from my father's house. He was always in his garage fixing his lowrider bicycle, listening to Oldies and smoking pot. Jessica hated him even then.

When she sold my dad's house, we moved into the apartments. I rarely saw him except when I ran into him around town. One time, I saw him late at night in front of a mini-mart. He was coming out of the store with some of his friends, who looked kind of hardcore cholo. They were getting into his car, four of them, and I nodded *what's up* to Freddy. "What's hanging, little man?" he said and got into the car.

Now he was driving me somewhere.

He laughed a hearty laugh and patted me on the shoulder. "You really want to know where I'm taking you?"

"Where?"

"Everland."

"Oh, yeah? Sounds magical. I can hardly wait."

"I have something to show you," he said, getting all serious.

"Why can't you just tell me?"

"It's a surprise."

We were at a red light, the windows down, and stopping next to us was a shiny new car with three pretty girls. They were listening to Maná or some other Mexican pop rock band, playing it loud on their stereo and dancing and singing in their seats. They looked like rich, Mexican girls that wouldn't give a normal Chicano like me a smile or a nod. Freddy saw them, too, and he leaned over me and yelled, "Hey, you girls want to go to a carnival? Follow us."

They hit the button to lift the automatic windows, and that drowned out his voice.

"They don't know what they're missing," he said.

The light tuned green and they drove off fast.

"Are we really going to a carnival?" I asked.

"I told you. We're going to Everland."

"Hey, can I ask you something? I don't remember much about the, you know, when I died."

"That's weird to say that, I bet. *When I died.*"

"Yeah, it feels kind of strange."

"I like the way that sounds," he said. *"When I died . . .* things were better back then. *When I died . . .* I was holding a flower. *When I died . . .* I was looking into your eyes. *When I died. When I died.* I could write a song like that."

"What were you doing with me?"

"I wasn't with you," he said. "I hadn't seen you in years, bro. I just happened to be driving by when those guys popped you."

He had been on his way somewhere. He was listening to some tunes, taking it slow, cruising at lowrider speed, when he looked into the Cherry Auction parking lot and saw boys fighting. Then he saw the gun go off—smoke from the barrel and a loud pop—and some of the boys ran away, got into a Hummer and drove off.

"A Hummer? Who drives a Hummer?" I asked.

"I don't know, man, but who were they? Why did they want you so . . . dead?"

"I don't remember anything."

"Come on! You must remember something."

I thought about it. "I might remember being on the ground, looking up at them surrounding me."

"Crazy, isn't it?" Freddy said. "I just *happened* to be driving by. It's like destiny. For some reason, you and I are connected. *¿Qué no?* I forgot all about you. Didn't even know where you lived, and now here we are, kicking it again, just like we used to in my garage. We're like soul homies."

"Uh, sure," I said.

"That's why I visited you in the hospital. *En serio.* Coincidental shit like that don't just happen, you know? Not without it meaning something. For some reason, you and I are connected."

He pulled over on the side of the street. He parked at a curb and stopped the engine. He shifted in his seat, facing me. He was silent for a while, looking at me, as if he was in love with me. It was kind of creepy.

"Can we pray?" he said.

"What?"

"Pray. I'd like to pray with you."

I didn't know if he was joking or not, so I sat there stunned, thinking of how I might escape from his car—*just open the door, fool, and run out!* He grabbed both my hands with a strong grip and he held them in his. Then he closed his eyes and bowed his head. "Heavenly Father," he said. "Please bless this journey we're about to take."

After he was done, he turned on the engine, and we drove off. "Now let's go kick some ass," he said.

And it turned out that he *was* taking me to a carnival.

It was on the campus of Fresno City College, some sort of education carnival for high school Chicanos from all over the city's high schools, from the hardcore barrios to the rich sides of town.

He led me through the carnival—past cute girls and game booths—to a courtyard with a fountain. They had set up a bunch of tables with pamphlets and free pens or post-it notes with the name of the college.

"What are you going to major in?" he asked me.

"Ars moriendi," I said.

"What the hell is that?"

"The Art of Dying."

"Art? Art it is," he said.

"No, maybe philosophy."

"Do a double major," he said.

I got a sudden whiff of popcorn coming from another booth where they had a machine going, and it smelled good.

He led me to a table and introduced me to the art majors, a boy and a girl, dressed like devil worshippers, all in black and red. The girl wore a pentagram necklace and the boy had on black make-up.

"This *vato* has had a hard life on the streets," he said, "but he's going to college and he's majoring in art."

"What kind of art do you do?" asked the girl.

"Do you draw?" asked the boy.

I shrugged and said, "Kind of."

"Cool," he said.

"That makes you an artist," said the girl. "Don't be embarrassed to call yourself that."

"That's right," said the boy. "Claim that term. Call yourself an artist."

"Uh, thanks," I said.

"A Chicano artist," Freddy said.

On the table they had a bunch of postcards of paintings.

"That one's cool," I said.

It was of this Mexican man looking off onto the horizon, where you could see fields and a line of barbed wire. He looked like he was tired.

"That's Maceo Montoya."

"Maceo Montoya," Freddy said, picking up the postcard. "That name sounds familiar."

"You can have the postcard," the boy said to me.

"Thanks," I said.

"Tell him about the contest," Freddy said.

They told me that there was an art contest to design the Cinco de Mayo flyer for the City College events. They handed me an entry form. To enter you had to be a high school student in the area. The winning image would be used on all the publicity material, posters, flyers. "Your art will be seen all over the city," said the girl.

"And here's the good part," said Freddy. "The winner gets 500 bucks."

"What??" I said.

"It's a scholarship," said the boy. "You have to use it for college."

"What's the drawing supposed to be?" I asked.

"Anything," the girl said. "Draw whatever Cinco de Mayo means to you. What matters is *your* vision," she said. "Don't let anyone tell you what you should draw. Your vision matters."

"Uh, okay."

All the Chicano college students that day were trying a little too hard to relate to me, as if they were generations older than me. I knew they meant well. They wanted to encourage at-risk Latino kids to go to college. Barrio boys like me needed to be saved, and they had the One and Only savior, *education.*

All the students gathered in a big theater. There were hundreds of kids. And there were banners all over about Chicano pride and anti-drug and anti-gang messages.

The messed up thing was, as I looked around at all the high school kids, none of them were even close to being gang bangers. They were regular kids. They weren't drug addicts or cholos or cholas. They were kids who already wanted to go to college.

The organizers, the college Chicanos, were preaching to the choir.

One of the first speakers was a college student named Ralphie.

He was short and stocky, dressed hip hop style. He even had a cap pulled backwards. He walked to the center stage in a cool hip hop stroll. He grabbed the microphone from the stand and like a DJ started yelling, *Gente in the house!*

Then he held up the microphone so the crowd could yell all excited.

Only they didn't yell all excited.

Just a few kids mumbled, *Yeah.*

That didn't stop Ralphie. He kept saying, *Raza in the house! Raza in the house!* Finally most of the kids must have felt sorry for him, so they clapped and cheered some. That seemed to make Ralphie pretty happy.

"That's more like it," he said, walking around in circles with the microphone, as if he imagined himself a rapper, trying to look all street.

"En serio," he said. He got silent, looked around at us. That was when I noticed that his two eyes looked off in different directions, that one eye didn't look at the same spot as the other.

"That's right. That's right. Check it out: When you look up here and you see me, you see a college student, right? I'm majoring in Criminology. That's right, and know what? In another year or so, I'll be transferring to Fresno State!!"

He paused, so the kids could cheer at the good news, but none did, only other college students, some of whom yelled, "Way to go, Ralphie!"

"I'm going places with my life."

He paused, his hand on his chest, his two eyes looking off in two different directions.

"But it wasn't always like this. Let me tell you. I was in the streets, man. I was into a hard life. I was into drugs. I went to parties. I was involved with gangs."

I laughed, and looked around to see who might be next to me, because I knew this kid had never been in a gang. I could tell.

"We're here to tell you that there's a better way."

Freddy went on next, and I guess he had known some of the kids, because they cheered for him as he walked on the stage.

He grabbed the microphone and said some of the names of the high schools that were there, yelling them out as if they were names of hometowns. That made kids scream, as if they were proud of their school. "You guys are here for a reason, man. You have a chance. You don't have to belong on the streets no more. You know what? *Say hello to my little friend*," he said in the voice of Al Pacino in *Scarface*.

He held up a piece of paper. "It's called a diploma. It's a little friend called education, and let me tell you, it saves lives.

"I want to tell you a story about a friend of mine, a *vato*, only fourteen years old. Man, this little homie has had it rougher than most people can even imagine. He lives in the barrio, man, and he was so involved in gangs and drugs and *la vida loca* that he was killed. That's right. He was shot dead. But you know what? He came back to life. I ain't playing: he rose from the dead. He was dead for like twenty minutes. Maybe you read about this in the papers. He was only dead for a little while, legally dead. I'll tell you right now, man, The Universe, Fate, God, whatever language you want to use. I like to say the Lord Jesus Christ. God said, *'Nah, little brother. It ain't your time.'*

"He came back to life! That's right. He was given another chance. That little brother is here with us today."

He was silent, so people could look around and wonder who it was.

One thing became clear: Freddy thought I was in a gang.

That was why he had picked me up. He wanted to save me. That was why they treated me so nice. I was the personification, in their eyes, of the Chicano boy who needed to be pulled from the life of the streets and into the classroom. They saw me and they saw a gang member who needed salvation. They saw a cholo, a thug.

I had noticed that every time he introduced me to other college students, he alluded to the crazy life that I led, and how I was too smart to waste away in the streets. He thought I was banger.

Kids were looking all around trying to see who the living dead might be, and then Freddy looked right at me, right into my eyes, and everyone else's eyes turned on me. They started whispering to each other, "That's him" and, "He looks like a banger." I had never felt so watched, and I didn't know what to do. My mind was confused in both thoughts and feelings, so my body took over.

I clenched my fists.

I felt my face burning, like I was about to go into a rage. I looked around at the people—all those faces looking at me, girls and boys, dark round faces with big eyes, skinny faces with long hair. Some people turned away when I looked at them, but I was slowly turning my head, so I could return the stares of everyone. I was spinning slowly around. When my eyes reached the eyes of others, some of them nodded to me or raised a fist in solidarity, as if we were on the same team. The few cholo-looking guys gave me a quick, cool nod, as if to say "Zup?"

"In a sense," Freddy's voice suddenly filled the entire room, blaring from all the speakers.

We all turned toward him.

He held the microphone like a preacher.

"In a sense," he repeated. "This is a story about all of you. All of you are dying in the barrios. You just don't know it. But all of you are also getting a second chance at life. And that's what we want you to know today. That's why we're here, working hard to get *you* here. We want you to have a second chance at life. Die to the streets, man, and wake up to a college education!"

Some people clapped and cheered.

"Let me see some hands. How may of you people are going to college? Raise your hand."

Some of the kids raised their hands, but not too enthusiastically. "Come on, let's see some hands!" Freddy yelled.

The other Chicano college students walked around yelling, *Come on!*

They were going up to kids and raising their hands for them.

Ralphie saw me and he stopped right in front of me. "Raise your hand, brother." He looked at me with one serious eye. It felt a little weird, because he was looking at me, but his other eye was looking away from me. "Come on, little brother!" I felt kind of bad for him, so I raised my hand. That made him happy, as if I had been saved. He grabbed my hand and raised it and yelled, *Yeah!*

People cheered.

❋❋ ❋❋ ❋❋

She wore a black tank top with an image of a lavender orchid, and across the chest it said "Opeth."

"So you're the guy that was killed?" she asked. She pulled long black hair behind her shoulder. It was straight, and her skin was dark brown. She looked Indian, not like an Apache, like me, but like someone from India. Her nose was a bit long, kind of crooked.

We were in the lunch line, waiting to get our free box, walking slowly, as the line moved fast.

"Was it cool?" she asked.

"What do you mean *cool?*" I asked.

"I think it would be cool. I mean, not the *getting-shot* part, or the *bleeding-all-over-yourself* part, or the *it-must-have-hurt-like-hell* part. But the twenty minutes part."

"He got it wrong. It was two minutes, two seconds."

"Still. It sounds like a cool experience. I mean, *death.*"

"Far out, man." I made the peace sign, and shook my head as if I couldn't believe what an idiot she was.

She squinted her eyes at me. "You don't have to be a jerk," she said.

I thought she was going to walk faster, go up further in the line with her friends, or go to the end, but she kept walking beside me, looking off at some trees that were passing by.

"Sorry," I said. "I didn't mean nothing."

"I didn't mean *anything,*" she said.

"You're correcting my grammar? That's kind of messed up."

"I'm sorry," she said.

"You're just like the rest of them."

"Rest of who?"

"You think I'm a dumb cholo that doesn't recognize a double negative?"

"All right! I'm sorry. Geeze. Don't get all bent out of shape. I ain't gonna correct you no more, okay?"

"Ain't?" I said.

"Ain't," she said.

"I be Victor." I offered her my hand.

"Me be Iliana," she said, shaking it like a business deal.

"Do you like death?" I asked, indicating her Opeth T-shirt. She shrugged and said, "You tell me. I never died. Not yet at least."

"You're T-shirt," I said. "You like Opeth? Death Metal?"

"Oh, this?" she looked down. "Actually, I just like the image."

As we walked, I could hear the sounds of conversations, laughter and distant doors opening and closing, but the most focused sound was our feet walking on the path, slowly to front of the line. I was dragging my shoes across the asphalt.

Walking, I sounded like a broom sweeping a floor. I saw my father standing in a doorway.

"So . . . was it cool?"

I shrugged. "I never thought of it that way."

We got our boxes and found a spot on the lawn with Freddy and another kid, who turned out to be her brother. His name was Pete, and he had a shaved head. Iliana and I opened our little white boxes at the same time, but I looked into hers and she looked into mine. We saw a sandwich on white bread, a bag of potato chips and a chocolate chip cookie. She looked at mine and looked at hers. She shrugged again and picked up the cookie.

She held it in front of me, inches from my face, and said, "Do you like cookies?"

I liked the way she said *cookies*.

"You can have mine," she said.

"Your what?" I said.

"My cookie."

"I'll take your cookie."

She handed it to me, like she was giving me a piece of herself, and I gobbled it up right away.

She leaned over her lap to unwrap her sandwich, doing it with such focus, like she was preparing a lab experiment. Her hair ran down her back.

"What do you know about Aztlán?" Freddy asked us. *"En serio,* what do you know about it? Aztlán. Does it sound familiar?"

Pete said something about the Aztecs, but I tuned him out and tuned in to Iliana.

She told me she was born in Mexico City. She was fourteen years old and liked old music, like Mars Volta, David Bowie. Her favorite poet was Sylvia Plath.

"You don't like Death Metal?"

"A bunch of noise," she said.

There was something about her voice that I liked. When she spoke, she sounded old, like a cynical adult, or a disenchanted teenager, like she didn't trust anything or anyone in the world. But at the same time, it was kind of innocent. When I asked her why she wanted to go to college, she said, *To be stinking rich.*

Although I knew she was joking, there was a kind of innocence in that she probably believed that college would be the answer to her dreams.

She told me that her parents spoke perfect English and Spanish, and so did she. Her mom's grandfather was from India, but by the time her mom was born, their family had lost their language and traditions and were 100 percent Mexican. She said that her father was also from Mexico, even though he looked like a white guy and his last name was Blum.

Iliana Blum.

Her name was Iliana Blum.

She asked what I remembered about death.

I looked around at all the people sitting on the lawn eating and I said, "Death? What was it like?"

"Yeah. Did you see anything? Hear anything? Did you see a white light?"

"Death," I said. I closed my eyes. I wanted to give her something, some detail, so I shut them tight and tried to remember. I thought about it hard, and I could feel my own effort like a weight pushing down on my body, but I couldn't get there. Nothing came to me. But somehow I knew there was a *there* there. Maybe dying wasn't something you did, but some place you went to, some place out of the body. I remembered the feeling like I was floating, like I was in a dark landscape hovering just above the ground and coming closer to a deep, black hole of swirling energy—that would suck me in and spit me out into a new light.

I saw myself entering into the emergency room, carried in the arms of Freddy. Maybe he was yelling, *My homie's been shot*, maybe blood all over his shirt, maybe the orderlies were pushing a bed up to him and Freddy put me on it. They pushed my bed down a hallway, wheels squeaking and spinning, people getting out of the way, doctors and nurses putting on their rubber gloves as they fast-walked alongside me, checking my vitals, and someone yelling, "We're losing him!"

Then it was nothing. Maybe I rose from my body.

Maybe when my heart stopped they looked at their watches or at a fat clock on the wall for the time of death and someone wrote the number on their clipboard and maybe the woman who wrote it down had neat handwriting like a schoolgirl. Maybe she had dark hair and dark skin and maybe she was Filipino and she shook her head as if to say *Too bad* and they put a sheet over my face.

I was floating, in slow motion, towards that black hole, and I remembered the word *Ain't*. I didn't remember it, I heard it. *Ain't*. Maybe someone had been whispering it around my deathbed, maybe Equis or my mom saying something like *It ain't true* as they looked over my dead body and the Filipino nurse tried to comfort them.

I opened my eyes. I was going to tell Iliana I couldn't remember anything, but in that moment right before I opened them, I remembered something else. The taste of fried cheese. Like the way cheese tastes when you're making an omelet and it seeps from the egg onto the pan and it gets brown.

She was looking at me, as if I had just gotten back from time travel. She put her hand on my leg. "Are you all right?"

"What do you mean?"

"Why were you saying *ain't?*" she asked.

"You asked me what I remembered about death. That's it. The word ain't."

"*Ain't?*"

"Yeah. That's what I remember."

"But *ain't*'s not a word," she said.

❧ ❧ ❧

By the end of the lunch hour, Freddy was surrounded by a bunch of kids sitting on the grass with him, as he talked about the Aztecs, how Cuauhtémoc's feet were burned in hot oil by Cortez, *pinche gringo*, who was a greedy bastard looking for gold. Pete, who had a Mexican education, knew as much or more about the Aztecs as Freddy, and occasionally he butted in to correct a detail in Freddy's story.

"Yeah, yeah! That's what I meant. Exactly! Thank you, little brother."

Then some college students walked around, from group to group, telling everyone to hurry up, because the workshops were starting.

We all stood up ready to go.

Pete went off with his friends to a workshop on the business major. Freddy had to be on a panel for another workshop he was doing on Chicano empowerment, so he took off, too, urging us to follow him. Most of the kids did follow him. He was like a Pied Piper, walking through the campus tailed by a rope of children.

Iliana and I stood on the hill watching people scatter away.

"Which workshop are you going to?" she asked.

"Advanced napping," I said.

"Let's go," she said.

We walked around a bit, looking for someplace to get away. But some college Chicanos saw us and shooed us into a workshop.

It was called 'Choosing a Major,' and it started by giving us a personality test. At first, I thought that it would be interesting to see what kind of person I was, but the test turned out to be stupid, with questions like:

On a Saturday night would you most rather do?

A) *Go to a party.*

B) *Stay home and watch a movie with a friend.*

C) *Read a good book by yourself.*

It was pretty obvious which answer would produce what result.

"This test is inane," said Iliana, leaning into me.

I liked the way she smelled. Like soap.

"You can get it to say whatever you want," I whispered.

"Yeah," she said. "I'm trying to get the test to say I would best be suited for disability checks."

"I want mine to point toward sales," I said.

"Like at Sears?"

"I'm thinking CDs at the flea market."

"Sweet," she said.

After the test, as we waited for the results, we looked around the room at the other high school kids.

I asked her what she thought she would really major in.

"Banana Peeling," she said. She nodded her head, acting all serious. "I'm going to be a Banana Peeler. What about you?"

"I'm going for Advanced Onion Slicing," I said. "I guess you could say there's more layers involved."

She punched me on the arm. "You're funny," she said.

"You think so?"

"Funny looking."

We skipped the next workshop and just walked around the college.

She told me she went to Clovis West.

"Clovis West?" I said. "You guys must be rich."

"Yeah, right?' she said. "Tell that to our landlord who's always pounding on our door for the rent check."

She had tiny earrings, each one a silver helix, always spinning around.

"So are you all into that Chicano stuff?" she asked.

I shrugged.

"You know what the Chicanos at Clovis West call me?"

"There's Chicanos at Clovis West?"

"*La* Hindu. Pretty racist, don't you think?"

"I guess."

"It exoticizes me."

She said the word *exoticize* as if the word itself were exotic.

"That makes me a double other," she said.

"Double other?"

"A Mexican *and* an Indian? In *Gringolandia*? I'm twice a minority. Thrice if you consider my sex."

"I'd be willing to consider your sex."

"I've had this discussion with my parents, and we all agree. My mother calls it *exoticization*. Well, she says it in Spanish, *exotización*. She says that's what *gringo* culture does to brown girls like me. Anyway, I'm just saying that it's racist to call me *la* Hindu. Don't you agree?"

"I'll think about it and get back to you."

"Make sure you do. In essay form. Double-spaced. Twenty pages."

"Can I email it to you? Or do I have to come all the way to Clovis to turn it in?"

"I don't care. You choose."

"Well, I want to make sure you get it. I mean, if I work hard on it."

"Do you have a car?"

"I'm fourteen."

"Couldn't you steal one?"

"We can wait until college," I said.

"Maybe we'll be college sweethearts."

"Yeah!" I said.

"We'll join a sorority and a fraternity."

"Yeah! I'll take you to the homecoming dance."

"I'll wear your letterman's jacket."

"I'll score you a touchdown."

"Or, we could not see each other until after we graduate college. Then we can skip the whole dating thing and college romance stuff and get married and have kids."

"How many kids do you want?" I asked.

"Fifty-seven," she said.

I laughed. "That's a funny number," I said.

Someone was walking by, and he looked our way. I waited until he passed. "What's wrong?" she asked.

"Nothing," I said.

We walked along the path, walled by the giant trees, and we passed a sunken garden.

She yelled, "Look!"

She ran down the stairs into the garden. I followed her. I ran like a child, my arms swinging out as if I had no control over them. But when I realized what I must have looked like, I held them in, closer to my body, like a football player jogging onto the field to play.

She got there first, and she stood in the open, dotted with sunlight and shade. The temperature seemed cooler down there, and she had spots of sun all over her face. A bunch of birds were singing while others flew from tree to tree, their shadows sliding across the ground.

"I don't know why," she said, "But I feel like doing *this!*"

She raised her hands, reaching into the sky as if she expected the sun would fall into her arms like a giant beach ball. "Come on! Join me. Do it!"

I stood next to her, and I looked up at the sun filtering through the treetops. I started to raise my arms like her, but I ended up using them to protect my eyes from the glare.

"Wouldn't it be cool if you could look into the sun?" she asked. "Wouldn't it? Without having to worry about burning your corneas? That would be so cool."

She lowered her arms. Then she looked around, as if looking for something fun to do.

"Let's do something," she said.

"What do you mean?"

"Let's play!" she said. Her eyes grew big, excited at the possibilities.

"Play?"

"What about hide and seek?" she asked. "When's the last time you played hide and seek?"

"When I was about five."

That seemed to disappoint her. She looked at me closely, like she was suspicious of me. "That's really too bad," she said. "I know. Let's pretend that we're in a secret garden. We can be fairies. Would you do that? Would you play a fairy if I asked you to?"

"What are you talking about?"

"You're too macho for that, huh?"

I walked across the open space to a bench made of stone and sat down.

"What is it with you Chicanos?" she said.

"What do you mean?"

"God, I hate it when guys try to be all macho."

It was sitting under some big tree, and suddenly a bird squealed from right above me.

"See, the bird agrees," she said, trying to look at it. "Chicanos suck," she said.

"I just don't want to play fairies, that's all."

"Okay, then do something gentle and sweet, something the opposite of macho. Just so I know."

"Fine." I pulled a small notepad out of my back pocket. I pulled out a pen, too. I looked up into the tree until I saw the little bird on a branch. I sketched it quickly. I even made the eyes look at the viewer, even if you moved the paper from side to side. I wrote across the top, "Iliana is a bird."

I ripped the drawing from the pad and gave it to her. She examined it. "Okay," she said. "I believe you." She slid the paper back and forth. "It stays looking at me! How did you do that?"

"I didn't. The bird did."

She folded the paper and put it in her back pocket.

I heard a bird squawk, and I turned around and saw bushes with blue flowers.

And flying over them were a few butterflies, their yellow wings filled with sunlight. Beyond the bushes there was a square of lawn. Iliana saw it and ran over there. I followed her. She stood in the middle of the green. I sat on another bench. Shading the lawn was a giant tree.

"Okay then. If you can't be a fairy, that's fine."

She picked up a leaf. She examined it closely, as if it were a treasure, then she put it to her ear. "Listen." She walked over to me. "Did you hear that?"

She put it to my ear.

"What am I listening for?"

"The People of the Leaf," she said. She kept it at my ear.

"Oh, yeah, I, uh, think I hear them."

"What are they saying?" she asked, serious-like.

"I'm not sure."

"Listen closer," she said. "Maybe you're the one!"

"The one?"

"For thousands of years the People of the Leaf could have been waiting for the one to come along, the only one who could hear their voices crying out. Listen, Victor! What are they saying? Help them." She looked so concerned, her big eyes blinking. "You must help!"

"Well, they probably know Horton," I said, pretending to listen to the leaf. "You know, the big elephant?"

"Of course I know Horton. We're good friends. I have his cell number."

"They're saying, *¡Aquí estamos!*"

She gently put down the leaf in a flowerbed. "You'll be safe here," she said. Then she turned around and faced me.

"Photography," she said.

"Huh?"

"That's what I'm really going to major in. I like taking pictures."

"You mean like a journalist?"

"Sure, why not? Whatever. I just want to take pictures."

She came and plopped down next to me on the bench. She was silent, looking around with wonder.

"I like it here," she said. "If I had to go to school here, this is where I'd do my studying."

"What do you mean if you *had to* go to school here?"

"Well, this wouldn't be my first choice now, would it?"

"I guess I never thought about that."

"You mean you're not going to college?"

"Who knows?" I said.

"Oh," she said.

She looked at a yellow flower on the grass. It must have been caught in a little breeze, because it was waving at her, and she waved back.

"You're not going to give me a speech about how I need college?" I asked.

"I don't care if you go to college," she said. "Just don't lose what makes you special."

"What's that?"

"I trust you," she said.

"What do you mean?"

She shrugged.

"My first choice is Berkeley," she said. "But if I had to go here, to City College, I'd study in this spot."

She got up and sat on the lawn.

She pretended she was surrounded by all her school-books. At least, I imagined she was pretending that.

"I see you surrounded by school books," I said.

"That's exactly what I was imagining! How did you know that? Victor, are you peeking into my heart?"

"Just a little."

"Not everyone can do that, you know. Most people think I'm mysterious and exotic."

"Most people think you're *la* Hindu," I said.

"Yes! Exactly."

"I see you have a laptop, too," I said, pretending to see it on the grass. "It's open." I pretended to look closely at it. "You're writing a paper."

"How did you know? It's on the history of US-Mexico relations. It's for Professor Pinkmayer's class."

"Professor Pinkmayor?"

"He's a very tough teacher." She pretended to type in some words. Then she stopped. "I'm tired of working."

She lay down across the lawn. "I'm taking a nap." She pretended to snore.

Then she stretched and yawned, as if she were just waking up, the tank top rising up her belly.

Then she looked at me.

She wiped her eyes with her fists. "Did I sleep long?"

"A thousand years," I said.

"I think my paper's going to be late."

"What will Pinkmayor say?"

She sat up. She lifted her hands and pretended she had a camera. She took a picture of me. "Click," she said. "To save for later."

And she clicked again. "So I don't forget you."

"Where's your real camera?" I asked.

"We can't afford one," she said, "but they promised they would get me one, and they just got me and my brother new laptops. My parents don't believe in credit. So if we don't have the cash, we don't get it. They're a little weird that way. They say they refuse to be like the rest of the sheep."

"Sheep?"

"That's what they call normal people. So for now, I borrow a camera from the school, when school is in session. During the summer I just pretend to have a camera." She stood up, and with her pretend-camera she took pictures all around the garden. She got a bird on a branch singing some song. She got a squirrel running up a tree, and she got another one on the lawn munching on a nut. She got a cluster of dandelions swaying like children back and forth on the grass. She got sunlight breaking through the trees. I followed her as she took her pretend pictures. "Click, click, click."

She stopped and looked at me. "You know, I almost believe that pretending to shoot pictures is as important as actually taking them. In some kind of weird way, it gives me another way of seeing."

She pointed the camera at me and said, "Click, click, click!" She moved closer to get a better imaginary shot of me. She was a few feet away from me, and when she held up the camera, her shirt rose a little further up her belly. She saw me looking. She clicked a picture of me. "Caught you," she said.

"I don't know what you're talking about."

"Want to touch my stomach?" she stepped back, lifted her shirt and showed me more belly.

I put my palm there.

"Can you tell I do sit ups?" she asked, flexing her stomach muscles. I felt them contract and harden in my hands.

"I'm just kidding," she said. "About the sit ups. I hate to exercise."

I'm not sure what happened next. I could have pulled her closer to me, or she could have walked closer to me (maybe both), but I put my arms around her. Her waist felt nice.

"Are you about to kiss me?" she asked. "That's kind of ballsy, don't you think?"

"You're weird."

"Yeah?" she said. "But not exotic, right?" She had grass and pine needles in her hair. I brushed some out.

She pretended to throw her pretend camera into the bushes. She looked at me, as if waiting for me to kiss her.

I moved in, but her brother came into the garden looking for her.

"The bus is leaving," he said.

"I'll be right there," she said, moving out of my arms.

"I guess this is it," I said.

"You're a nice guy," she said. "I'm glad I met you."

"Me too," I said.

I watched her run away with her brother, up the steps, onto the path, into the tall tress that lined it. "Iliana!" I yelled.

She stopped. She turned around and ran back to me. She ran down the stone steps into the garden.

"Yeah?" she said.

"Maybe I can call you," I said.

"You know about the Cherry Auction?" she asked.

"Yeah, the Saturday flea market. What about it?"

"My mom and dad set up a booth and sell their stuff. My dad's an inventor, I guess you could say. He gets these ideas that he thinks will make him a million dollars, and he sells them at the flea market."

"What kind of ideas?" I asked.

"Well, for example, last Saturday, we spent the whole day selling his frog colony. I know, it's weird, but he made this little frog community, because apparently frogs have good eyes, like a lot more effective than humans. So he made this colony of tiny frogs with bulging eyes. The kind that live in water, and he put it behind glass, in a bubble. The idea is that you have these frog eyes in your house, always watching you. I guess, with observers, you're supposed to act differently. He thought it was a good idea."

"That's strange," I said.

"Yeah, well my parents aren't what you would call typical."

"Come on!" yelled Peter from outside of the garden.

"Anyway, I'm out there on Saturdays. Every Saturday," she said. "Meet me there, okay?"

She kissed me on the lips, "Bye." Then she turned and ran away.

"Where at the Cherry Auction?" I yelled.

"By the big, white booth where they sell the world's best *churros*," she yelled.

"World's best *churros*," I repeated, watching her disappear underneath the line of trees and into a cluster of brick buildings.

On the drive back home, Freddy was trying to get me to think about what I might be able to draw for the Cinco de Mayo contest.

"It doesn't matter what it is," said Freddy. "Just something *bien* Chicano."

"*Bien* Chicano," I repeated. "Something very Chicano."

"That's right."

"Freddy, I like that girl, man, you know Iliana?"

"You mean *la* Hindu?"

"I mean Iliana."

"She's a good girl," he said, nodding his head all serious-like. "You guys hit it off, huh?"

"Yeah, we did. She's hella cool."

"What are your intentions?"

"What, are you her father?"

"Every Chicanita is my sister," he said.

"I like her," I said. "I mean, she's smart. She's good-looking." I pictured her pretending to take pictures, *click, click, click.* "I just like her, all right?"

He pulled up in front of my apartment. "All right, little brother. Tell your momers I said hi."

"I'm not allowed to see you, remember?"

"I thought you was joking," he said.

"No. She thinks you're why I was shot."

"That ain't right. Did you tell her the truth?"

"I don't really remember it all."

"That's messed up."

"Sorry," I said.

I left him there and went up the stairs to the apartment.

I was disappointed to see who was standing right outside the door waiting for me, almost too drunk to stand up.

※ ※ ※

Equis saw me coming and he held out his arms. "Hey, man!"

He looked all messed up. "Hey, man!" He stumbled toward me. "Where the hell have you been, bitch?"

"Equis, what the hell?"

I opened the door, and he fell into the apartment. He laughed and reached up, like someone burning in hell trying to grab at something. "Help me up, man!"

I pulled him to his feet. But once standing up, he could barely keep his balance.

"What are you doing?" I asked. "You can't come here like this."

"Give me some weed," he said, and pulled a metal pipe from his pocket.

"Not until you quit acting like a punk."

He stumbled over to the table and sat down, plop. "Damn. This place is hella weird." He looked around the apartment, as if it was haunted.

"You got to get out of here, Victor. I'm serious, man. There's something wrong with this place."

As he spoke, he kept patting his pockets, and then he pulled out a twenty. "Here, man," he said waving it in front of me. "Give me a small bag."

I grabbed the money and went to my bedroom. Without turning on the lights, I walked to the closet, reached up on the top where I kept the stash. I pulled out a twenty bag.

I wasn't a drug dealer.

I just couldn't afford to buy it unless I sold a little on the side, just enough so that it paid for itself.

When I got back to the couch, Equis was trying to suck on his pipe to get whatever resin remained inside the bowl. "Calm down," I said.

I threw the bag at his chest. At first he acted as if I had thrown a rock at him, but then he saw the plastic baggie on his chest and got all happy. He opened it and smelled it as if it was a good wine. He seemed happy as he pulled some leaves off the bud and stuffed them into his pipe.

"Not here," I said. "My mom'll be home any minute."

He pulled out his lighter, flicked and brought the flame to his pipe. I squeezed his cheeks, like he was a disobedient kid. His lips puckered up. "You don't do this now, you hear me? You're disrespecting my mom."

I nodded his head for him, and then I let go of his cheeks with a little push. I wiped my hands on my pants. He held his face as if it hurt.

"I'm sorry, dog," he said.

"You got to go."

That was when the knife fell out of his pocket.

"Are you still carrying that thing?" I asked.

He opened it and pretended he was in a knife fight. "We need this for the gang."

"Gangs use guns, *menso*. They'll shoot you in the head before you even pull it from your pocket."

"Our gang's gonna have style," he said, twisting and turning the knife in his hand like a showman.

"What gang?"

"Don't you 'member? We were at the Cherry Auction when those guys wanted to fight us, and you said we should jump in? 'We'll get girls,' you said. 'And those guys won't mess with us,' you said."

"Cherry Auction? What guys?"

"The guy that killed you."

"He was at the Cherry Auction?"

"You were talking to his girlfriend. Don't you 'member nothing?"

"Why didn't you tell me this before?"

"I thought you 'membered."

"I told you I didn't remember anything. I've been telling you that."

"But that was *before*," he said. "That was a long time before they shot you. You mean, you don't remember stuff before either?"

"Sure, I do," I said, but I wasn't sure. A rush of fear flowed through me and I tried to find a memory of what my life was like before dying, but all I could think of was drawing.

Then it came back to me as clear as a film clip. We were walking through the Cherry Auction, acting all cool, and near one of the food stands we were talking to some girls. One of them liked me, her name was Lili, and she had glitter on her cleavage. Her cholo boyfriend, or a guy who thought he was her boyfriend, came over with two other guys and they wanted to fight. Equis started his prefight movements, like he was loosening his bones. He'd shook his arms and legs like a kung fu fighter warm up, and he twisted his neck like a dog shaking off water. I remembered that Equis was a good fighter. Then I remembered that I was a good fighter. I remembered I said to Lili's cholo, "Come on, let's go," and we were about to go at it, but the cops came by and saw the other boys were wearing colors. The cops took them away and the guy yelled to me that he would get me.

I was so confused that I plopped down on the couch.

Equis came over and plopped down next to me.

"Those guys got arrested," I said.

"Yeah, and he said he would get us. When we was kicking it with Lili and those girls at her house that one guy showed up. Yeah, and that guy started challenging you."

And I went out on the front lawn and told him to get lost. He backed off, but he had a mouth on him and he started talking about how his homies were going to come and kick my ass and I told him he could bring as many as he wanted. He had a silver tooth and he was ugly, I mean, smashed-in face like a pug dog, and he was yelling a lot as he walked backwards and I walked forward. I got close enough to punch him hard, and he fell on the ground but he shot right back up and his mouth was bleeding so much you couldn't see his teeth when he yelled at me that I would die. The girls came out of the house and told us that we better get going, because a bunch of bangers were on their way and they would shoot us down. I felt heroic. I kissed Lili goodbye.

"On the way home you told me that we really would jump in and I should find out how to go about it. I should do research, you said."

"I was joking," I said. "I have no desire to be in a gang."

"Sometimes I don't know when you're joking, Victor. I'm serious. Maybe you think I'm stupid or something, but I don't know when you're joking or you're serious. You got some sort of . . . weird sense of humor."

"Get out of here, Equis."

"All right, bro. Mind if I take a leak first?"

"No, get out of here."

His acne looked especially bad on his neck, red and pink and moist. "I'm gonna piss my pants."

"Hurry up."

He stood up and stumbled his way to the bathroom.

A thought stopped him mid-step.

He turned around, walked toward me and gave me a hug. He smelled like booze, like he had been drinking for days. His clothes smelled like cigarettes.

"You're my number one homie," he said. Then he patted me on the back and hugged harder. "I'm sorry."

"Hurry it up," I said, pushing him away.

"All right," he said. He stood at attention like a soldier and did the salute, but he almost fell over. Then he turned around with a lot of effort and concentration, and he went into the bathroom, laughing all the way.

What came next is like a dream. I heard the cigarette lighter going on in the bathroom, and I knew he was taking hits, and I knew it wasn't pot. I pounded on the door ready to bust it down, but he was so messed up he hadn't even closed it. It swung open. He was smoking little white rocks in a pipe and the white-white smoke filled the room. I pulled him out and dragged him across the floor. The smoke must have reached the alarm, and it went off—a piercing electric beep. He got loose of me and stumble-ran down the hallway and we both fell onto the floor of my bedroom. I hit him with an open hand, like a father beating his child and he just clenched his face muscles to receive my blows.

He pushed me off of him and we stood up. He pulled the knife from his waist and raised it to my face.

"Stop hitting me!"

I could see it all as if I was out of my body watching from a distance, our two bodies facing each other, Equis pointing a knife at my face.

"Equis?" I said.

I saw him throw the knife on the bed and say, "I ain't going to do nothing."

I imagined some guy pointing a gun at my face saying "die" and I passed out.

Images flashed on and off, Iliana's face, treetops writing in the clouds, kids making a castle from cardboard boxes, Equis wearing his space helmet as he sits on his bed, legs crossed. Then the face of the boy who killed me came back, but he dissolved into particles of light. I had to squint my eyes, it was so bright. *What the hell are you doing here, boy?*

Here's the facts (as I would later put them together): I passed out. My mom saw the knife, and nothing would convince her that it wasn't mine. Later on that night, she found Equis' pipe in the bathroom, along with the rocks. Hard drugs. All I had ever done was smoke a little weed, but she thought that I had passed out because I was high on hard drugs. I tried to tell her the truth, but she wouldn't listen.

She not only sent me to La Malinche in Modesto, but she also made it clear that if I got into the slightest bit of trouble over there, if I didn't completely do whatever my *tía* told me to do, if she heard even one complaint from her, she would give up on me.

"I mean it, Victor," she said to me as she drove me to the downtown bus station, my bags in the backseat, my ticket to Modesto in hand. "I'll be through with you for good."

"What do you mean by that?" I asked.

"Don't make me show you what I mean."

I didn't know if she meant that she would send me to live with her family in Mexico, or if she meant that she would never see me again, but I knew she was serious. Disowning family members ran in her family.

PART TWO
THE CHERRY AUCTION

La Malinche was waiting for me at the bus terminal. She was a tall woman with short, salt and pepper hair. She wore jeans and cowboy boots and looked strong, like she could lift things. She had her hands on her hips like a cowboy. "Well look how you shot up!" she said in an accent that sounded more Okie than Mexican.

She walked over to me with her arms out, as if I were a guest. She gave me a big hug and patted my back like a man. "Look how big and handsome you are. Like an Indian prince. Your mama still call you Apache?"

"Not too much," I said.

"Those the only bags you got?" she asked.

I had a suitcase and a sports bag.

"Yes, ma'am," I said.

She grabbed my bag, carried it out to the parking lot, led me to a pickup truck and tossed my suitcase into the back. The truck was so tall I had to crawl up into the cab like a kid. "This your truck?" I asked.

"Had it since it was a puppy."

We drove out of the downtown bus terminal, which looked like all the other Valley downtown bus terminals: homeless people begging; skinny, crack-addicted men and women walking around like zombies. A muscular,

Chicano man leaned against the wall, arms crossed, dark sunglasses, tattoos all over his arms and neck, like he had just got out of prison.

La Malinche was listening to southern rock. She raised the volume.

Lord, I was born a rambling man!

"Do you like this music?"

"Yeah, sure," I said.

She sang the entire song as we rambled through town, stopping at red lights and swerving around all the traffic. Every now and then she looked my way, looked at me closely, like she was deciding something about me.

She lowered the volume. "Now listen. I'm gonna fill you in on how things are going to work around here, okay? Johnny's home for the summer, but he's working on his projects and running his business. I'm gone all day at work, and most of my weekends are booked solid for the next three months, so he's going to be in charge. Okay? You got to listen to whatever he says. But don't worry, he's a good kid, a very responsible young man."

"What kind of work do you do?" I asked.

"I got a temporary job," she said. Then she started singing, *Lord, I was born a rambling man.*

"I help a family run their dairy. One of the few independent farms left around here. Everything else has been bought up by mega corporations. Dairy Godoy it's called. That's the name of the man that owns it, Godoy, a Mexican from Michoacán, barely speaks English. He started out as a laborer and ended up buying his own land, he and his wife Elida and two of the cutest little kids you can imagine. Forget their names. María's one of them, I think. Or maybe she just looks like a María. Anyway, we make milk and butter and sell it to companies that pack-

age and distribute it under their own label. Unfortunately, all of them that buy our product are big companies.
But what can you do? At least the farm itself stays belonging to Godoy and María. I mean, Elida. Even if they don't
have their own label. Those big corporations have been
trying to get at him for years."

"How long have you been working there?" I asked.

"About ten years."

"I thought you said it was a temporary job," I said.
"Ten years doesn't sound temporary."

"Yeah, well, nothing is forever. Just remember that.
It'll save you from a lot of disappointment in life."

"Yeah, I guess nothing is permanent, huh?"

"Only change," she said.

Today, the day I arrived in Modesto, was Saturday.

Iliana must have been at the flea market, and I imagined her walking back and forth in front of the *churro*
booth looking for me. The Cherry Auction must have
been packed. I saw her walking alone, but the scene
around her started to fade out into particles and only she
remained standing among swirls of black and red.

"So how's your mother?" La Malinche asked.

"Pissed off."

We were at a stoplight. La Malinche was looking at me
real close. I looked back at her too, but not for long. Her
gaze was strong. She patted my thigh. "You're not in a
gang, are you?"

"No, but my mom thinks I am."

"I used to do volunteer work with gangs. That's one of
the reasons she thought I could help you."

She looked at me like she was examining me. "You're
not a gang member. At least not yet."

I looked out the window, because I didn't want her to see the cherry trees in my eyes.

"You got a lot of rage in you."

"I do not."

"I'm not saying you don't have love inside of you—you have a lot of that I can tell. I'm pretty good at sizing people up. I don't think you're a bad kid at all. I just think you have some anger in you. Maybe more than you realize. And it keeps getting you into trouble. But, *m'ijo*, all you need is a little Productive Activity."

"What's that?"

"Productive meaningful stuff to do. It worked for Johnny. That's how I raised him. First thing you'll probably notice about our house is that we don't have a TV set. Know why?"

"TV's a waste of time?"

"But you'll find lots of books and, well, Johnny's stuff."

We drove past storefront buildings and vacant lots and approached a wall that ran parallel to the street, tall as a building, and it went on for what seemed like miles.

"What's that?" I asked.

"A big old winery. I used to work there. That's why I moved back to California from the beautiful north, to take a job with those jokers. I quit after two years."

"How come?"

"Quick answer: Too corporate for me. Long answer: Let's talk about an entity whose mission it is to enslave the poor. Keep them drunk."

We drove on, and the wall went on and on. It curved along with the bends in the street, like the Great Wall itself, and every half mile or so there appeared a door in the wall, a red metal door onto the street. I wondered about the kingdom on the other side.

"So you really died, didn't you?" asked my aunt.

"That's what they say. 122 seconds."

"See a white light?"

"I'm not sure. Maybe. Or something like that. Maybe. Don't really remember."

"Did you see your father?"

"Maybe," I said. I thought about it and what came to me was the taste of cheese. "Every time I try to remember being dead, something comes to me. I'm not sure if it's from the time I was dead or of it's just something passing through my thoughts right now."

"What kind of thoughts?"

"The taste of fried cheese."

"Really?"

"Yeah, weird I know. But I think I remember tasting cheese."

"Well, that's encouraging. Death can't be so bad if you get fried cheese."

"I don't think I saw anything."

"Not even light?"

"I don't know. I saw things with my gut."

She nodded her head, as if she understood, but then she asked "How so?"

"I could hear color."

"That's very deep, Victor."

"There's a philosophy called *ars moriendi*. The art of dying," I said. "I guess I'm not a very good artist."

She pulled into a little neighborhood that looked even worse than ours. The houses were poor and there were apartments scattered here and there. I could tell there were gangs around, and I laughed at the irony. My mom wanted to take me out of one gang place, and she put me in another. Maybe she pictured her sister's life as somehow more ideal, because she owned her own house and her son was attending Berkeley.

"One other thing," she said.

She pulled her truck into a gravel driveway. She turned toward me, as if she were going to tell me something important. "There's going to be random searches of your stuff, just to make sure you're keeping clean, okay? I know you're a good kid. You're smart and probably every subject in school is boring to you. I see it in you, Victor, but you're also into things you shouldn't be into."

"Those rocks weren't mine. I don't do hard drugs."

"Maybe not, but you're street smart. Smart and street smart: that could be a dangerous combination, or it could be your strength as well. Quite frankly, you need perspective."

I had a small amount of weed in my bag, wrapped up tight inside rolled up socks. I wondered if she could smell it. It smelled like skunk, but there was such a small amount that I figured it wouldn't stink. I involuntarily looked back down at my bag, a black sports bag with Nike across the side. It was a bootleg brand that I had gotten at the flea market.

My aunt jumped out of the truck, pulled my fake Nike from the floor and led me to the house. "Let's go," she said.

"I'll take that, Tía," I said.

"Call me Che," she said. "And I got it. I ain't that old."

Before we got to the door, I heard someone's voice talking, low-pitched, saying, "the unification of these forces imply some sort of aggressive shift . . . "

We walked in, and the voice was louder, coming from a speaker. " . . .such labyrinthine logic . . . "

The place looked like a computer repair workshop. There were computers and laptops everywhere. There were tables and desks pushed against the walls, and all over the surfaces were papers and books and open laptops and computer parts and old computers—their screens giving off dull, iron-colored light. One desktop computer was down-streaming the voice we were hearing. " . . . emphatic receptions of opposites . . . "

The walls had notes pinned to them, articles cut from magazines and newspapers, and a bunch of scribbled numbers. It looked like the office of some mad genius. All the while, that voice kept going on and on " . . . they can call it what they want—use whatever euphemism suits their platform, but the facts are reflected not in rhetoric but in math. Numbers don't lie. They reveal."

The room must have once served as a living room. It was narrow and long, reaching all the way to a large window at the end, which let in some light in spite of the blue sheet that had been hung over it to keep out the sun.

There was a copy machine in one corner, and there were a few fax machines on wobbly worktables and a stack of wireless routers, the cords wrapped around them.

"I'm afraid Johnny's business has taken over most of the house," she said.

There were so many office swivel chairs that it looked like a headquarters for a think tank.

There was no TV, no couch, no armchair, no ottoman, no cute paintings on the walls, no sense of a living room.

"Johnny! Your cousin's here!" she yelled.

" . . . who's responsible for the majority of journalist killings and other innocent lives? Many analysts have predicted . . . "

Then the voice turned off.

"I'm busy right now," someone yelled.

Only then did I notice that at the end of the room, to the left of the blue blanket on the window, was another room, where the voice was coming from. I could see a shadow moving on the wall.

"That's Johnny," she said to me.

Then the shadow appeared at the end of the living room, blocking out the window. I could make out the form of a big body. I couldn't see a face, just a huge silhouette of a man.

"Honey, can you say hello to your cousin Victor?" she said.

"The gangbanger?" he said. "Watch your purse. And make sure you hide the valuables."

I stepped forward. "That's messed up," I said, looking at him, but I couldn't see his face.

"Be nice, Johnny," she said.

"For Christ's sake, Mother! He's a cholo."

And then his shadow slowly moved back into the other room, like a giant bear going back into his cave.

※ ※ ※

"Come on," she said. "I'll show you your room."

She took my bag in the opposite direction. We passed through the kitchen. On the eating table, there were stacks of books and another open laptop. There were bookshelves in the kitchen with hundreds of books, and I wondered where they kept their food.

My room turned out to be a one-car garage that had been converted into a bedroom. Kind of converted. It was narrow and the walls were made of plasterboard. The floor was cement. There was only one window. It looked out onto a covered porch glowing in green sunlight, because the roof of the porch was made of green plastic. The porch was full of junk: old copy machines, printers, computer screens so huge they must have been from back in the days when computers were new. I could picture a bunch of cave people looking into those giant monitors. There was also a stack of desks and chairs that looked like they had come from an old elementary school. There were metal filing cabinets, the gray-colored kind you would find in old government offices. There were old telephones and office machines that I didn't even recognize. I guessed they were the machines Johnny kept around for extra parts, things that in themselves had no use. There was a pile of electric adding machines, the kind that used rolls of paper to print out numbers. There was even a huge abacus, but some of the beads were missing, and next to it, there was a bucket of loose beads.

"Sorry we can't get you a better place," Che said.

My bed was a military cot, a thin strip of green canvas stretched over wooden sticks. There was a stack of blankets and pillows on it.

"That bed's not so bad if you use one of those comforters as a mattress. It gets kind of hot in here, but there's a fan."

There was a chest of drawers painted a faded green, and the empty drawers were sticking out like tongues. The fan stood on the chest of drawers, a metal fan like a prop from an LA detective movie set in the 1930s, the blades set on low. The shadows of the blades moved slowly along the wall like a ghostly parade of elephants.

"And look, you got a radio!"

On an upside-down plastic milk crate—with a pillowcase thrown over it like a table cloth—was a clock radio, the red LEDs blinking the time.

"It's got both AM and FM," she said.

There was a bucket next to the bed, which Che grabbed, turned upside down and sat on.

"Sit down," she said. I sat on the cot, which sunk in from my weight. I felt like my butt was almost touching the floor.

I looked on the wall, and there were a bunch of notes, scribbles of words and numbers.

"This used to be Johnny's office," she said. "He started his business out of here when he was fifteen years old. He goes to junkyards and buys office machines and computer parts. Then he fixes them up and sells them for ten times what he paid. Fortunately, Berkeley gave him a bunch of scholarships. Basically he got a full ride. He hasn't asked money from me since he was sixteen, and he pays his share of the bills. And now—during the summer—he's taking online courses *and* running his business at the same time. It's killing him. That's why he's so grumpy."

She looked around the room and sighed.

"This just isn't enough room for him anymore." She thought of something, and then she laughed. "I guess I could mean that literally, too. He gained a lot of weight since he's been at school. I suppose you noticed he's a big boy. I try and tell him he should go on a diet, but he won't listen. He loves his junk food. That's all he eats. Don't tell him I'm telling you all this."

She looked around the room.

"Used to park my '69 Impala in here. Johnny was just a baby."

I pictured the room as a garage, oil on the floor, the garage door opening, a Chevy Impala slowly pulling in.

She told me that I would be helping Johnny with his business.

I was to do whatever he wanted me to do.

"You'll probably help him fix the machines and stuff. It may seem like useless work to you, but I tell you, this could be a good summer for you. You need to find something in life that interests you more than girls and having fun with your friends. You need to hone your focus skills. Always remember: Focus is power."

"I don't understand."

"All rightie. Think of the Law of Conservation of Energy. You know what that is?"

"No."

"Well, you see, one of the laws of nature tells us that energy never disappears. It's just converted into other forms of energy. For example, when a person falls from a tall building—say like the Empire State Building, going down that fast with all that gravity and mass. That's energy. Kinetic energy. When you hit the cement on the bottom, the energy that comes from that motion doesn't go away. It's converted into heat and friction from the impact, and that's why you splatter into a million pieces. Well, this is just a law of nature. You're made of energy, Victor. We all are. If you put your energy into something special, some task—and I don't mean chasing girls or getting into fights—then that focus intensifies the energy, which is power. If you know how to focus your intention, you can do whatever you want. That's where Productive Activity comes in. We're going to help you get focused."

I felt like I was becoming numb, empty, floating in nothingness. I had no energy. It was hot in that room. My energy must have been converted into something else. Maybe the heat in the room was me.

She stood up, patted me on the head and said, "Tomorrow, at 7 a.m. we'll have breakfast together. Set your alarm clock. I'll see you then. Don't be late. That'll upset Johnny, and you don't want to do that. One word from him, and I have to send you back to your mom. I don't think she'd be too happy."

"What if he doesn't like me?"

"That shouldn't matter. It's in his best interest that you stay all summer."

"Why's it in his best interest?"

"Let's just say we made a deal."

She left me alone in the room.

I looked at the clock radio. It was only 7 p.m., still bright and sunny outside.

I quickly unzipped my Nike bag, took out the rolled up socks and looked around for a place to hide my stash. I saw that the wooden beams were still exposed on the ceiling, so I got the bucket, turned it over and stood on it. I reached up to hide the stash up there in the rafters.

Then I pushed the bucket back where it had been and sat down on the cot.

I guess I was expected to stay in that room until the next day.

I lay on the cot and looked at the ceiling. I stared at the wooden beams. I pictured myself hanging by a rope from one of them.

※ ※ ※

"Hey," I said. "Good morning." I was standing in the kitchen doorway.

I had set the alarm for 6:45 a.m.

"Well, look who's up!" said Che. She looked at her watch. "Right on time." She turned to Johnny. "I told you!"

Johnny was seated at the table filling a huge bowl with sugary cereal. He emptied out what was left in the box, and then shook it to listen for stray pieces.

"Hi, Johnny," I said.

I walked over to shake his hand, but he was shaking the box, trying to get the pieces out, the Captain's upside down face blurring back and forth over the mountain of cereal already in the bowl. "Can we skip the formalities?" he said.

He looked like the Comic Book Guy on *The Simpsons*.

He had long, dirty blonde hair and he was fat, even his face. His cheeks jiggled as he talked. He wasn't big like Freddy was big. Freddy was solid, strong. This guy was soft, and he wore huge T-shirts that stretched across his belly and dirty sweatpants, the kind with elastic around the ankles.

"Do you have experience working with computers?" he asked.

He poured milk into his bowl and stirred everything around with a big spoon.

I mumbled, "Not really."

"I'm sorry," he said. "I don't speak cholo. I asked if you have any experience working with appliances. Computers? Anything?"

"I don't think so."

"You either do or you don't," he said.

"My mom has a computer," I said, which I knew right away was a stupid thing to say, and sure enough, he dropped his spoon as if surprised by my answer. "What? Are you that dense? I don't care if you have enough skills to check email!"

"Johnny, be nice."

"Maybe he could scrub floors," Johnny said.

"No, you got to give him mind-expanding work," she said. "That was the deal."

"Yes, but in this case there's very little mind to expand," he said.

"You hush now," she said. "You will not mistreat that boy."

I looked down at my clenched fist and realized I wanted to kick his ass. I mean, really badly. Later, I thought maybe my aunt was right, maybe I had a lot of anger in me, because my face was red. I was ready to pounce.

I spent all my waking hours with Johnny. He never watched TV or read a book just to read it. He didn't have any friends or go on dates. The only interaction he had with other people was when someone came over to buy something he had advertised on Craigslist. He was impatient with his customers, explaining how to use a machine as if they were idiots. People seemed to hate him instantly.

He seemed so indifferent to other peoples' feelings that he must have enjoyed doing it. No one could *not* care that much, or so I thought. Years later, I would think of him and wonder if he had autism, if he was one of those beautiful minds that can focus on numbers and details like a genius but has no clue what others are feeling. All day he sat at a table hunched over a machine, taking it apart and rebuilding it with such precision and attention, such intense focus. He tried to teach me how to fix things, leaning over me like a humid tent. He tried to show me how to take out a hard drive, how to test a battery, how to change wires and cables, but he stunk like fart and fried meat, and I had to hold my breath because it made me gag.

I made a lot of stupid mistakes on purpose, and he'd call me a hopeless idiot and tell me to go away. I was happy when he gave me a job away from him. One day, he told me to go out back to the patio and clean it up.

I made it a week-long project, happy to be away from him.

I made stacks of like machines, fax machines with fax machines, answering machines in one pile, copy machines pushed off to one corner of the patio. I dusted the filing cabinets, wiped clean the screens of computer monitors. But mostly, I wasted time just so I wouldn't have to go inside. I picked up machines, looked at them and put them down in another spot.

One afternoon, I peeked through the sliding glass door and saw him inside with his nose glued to a computer screen. He looked focused, so I knew he could be in that position for hours. I went to my room. I scooted the bucket underneath the ceiling beams and took out my stash.

I only took a few hits, so I put it out and hid it in my sock. I knew Johnny could walk out any minute and I didn't want to get caught. He wouldn't understand. He'd think I was doing drugs, and he'd send me back to Jessica.

She would send me off somewhere far, maybe Mexico to live with her family. I could imagine myself in Chihuahua, doing whatever they did there, watering goats from a tin bucket, riding a horse to the stone church, meeting a girl in the dusty plaza and buying her a *churro*. I pictured Iliana dressed like a traditional Mexican girl, a white dress and red bow in her hair. I held her hand and whispered something in her ear and she laughed.

Everything was shaded a tint of green, even my arms, because of the patio roof cover, that slab of green plastic. I looked at my hands, and they were green.

Verde, que te quiero verde.

I was green. I saw a box with yellowed index cards. I pulled one out and held it up. It was green. *My green card,* I said to myself and laughed.

I looked at both sides of the index card. There was no writing. I wanted to draw. I looked around for a pen or pencil.

Green hands. Green fingernails.

I was an alien from outer space, and the patio was the bridge of my spaceship, all those gadgets, the machines that go *bling!* The computer screens and keyboards, the dials and levers. I was on my way to planet Earth. "Coordinates for Earth," I ordered my crew member. His name was QzxQttfg, and he had a single antenna coming from his head and three eyes. He was a Bagolog, a species that had no nose and a tiny mouth that made his voice squeaky when he spoke.

"Are you sure you want Earth, Captain?" he asked. "No one has ever dared to go there. They say the humans are not friendly."

"To Earth!" I said.

I sat in a wobbly office chair, spun it around and adjusted some controls on what used to be a military radio, the kind you talk into with a desktop microphone. I spoke into it. "Crew, prepare to land on Earth. Be on alert. We don't know what to expect from these creatures, but my guess is you better be ready to fight! Prepare your laser guns."

I was surrounded by weird looking guys like QzxQttfg, all of them running around preparing to land. Some of them were female, and the Bagolog species differed greatly according to gender. The women all wore green tights, and they had heads like humans, only green.

I spoke into the microphone. "I'm asking for volunteers to come to Earth with me. No one has to leave the ship, but I'm going out there to explore. I want to know about these Earth people. Any volunteers?"

QzxQttfg stood before me, his single antenna dangling on his head. He looked like a Star-bellied Sneetch. He saluted me, and said, "I'll go with you, Captain."

"You sure?"

Next to him stood another crewmember, a female. She was cute. "Me too, sir. I'd like to go with you."

"What's your name?"

"R%7G*/eqxz," she answered.

"Wha?"

"You can call me Quark."

Verde que te quiero verde.

"All right, here we go!" I said. "Prepare to land!"

I shook in my chair as if it were a bumpy landing. I slid around the floor on the wheels. It was a rocky landing, but we landed right in the middle of a Walmart parking lot.

We saw hundreds of Earthlings go in and out of the wide glass doors, going in with nothing but coming out pushing metal carts full of stuff.

"What do you suppose it is, Captain?" asked Quark.

She had her hand on my shoulder and was bent over me looking at my screen. "I'm not sure," I said.

※ ※ ※

That was when I heard the sliding glass door swoosh open, and Johnny came out the house looking for a part.

"What in God's name are you doing?" he said.

I was embarrassed to be caught playing like a kid, but he was looking around at how I had arranged everything, his hands on his hips like a foreman. He hadn't even noticed that I had been playing.

"I won't be able to find a thing out here."

"I'm just organizing things," I said.

"You were supposed to clean, not rearrange my stuff. You better get inside the house. I'll find something even more brainless for you to do."

He started to look around for the part that he needed, but he suddenly froze. He stood up straight and flared his big nostrils, sniffing for something. "What's that smell?" he asked, more to himself than me.

"What smell? There's no smell."

He kept taking big whiffs with those huge nostrils of his.

Then he looked at me. "What have you been doing?"

"I don't know what you mean."

"You've been smoking pot!"

"You're crazy," I said.

"Yes, you have, you little . . . "

"Little what?"

"Little stoner!"

"It's probably the neighbor. It must be coming from over the fence."

"She's an eighty-year-old woman who can barely walk," he said. "Let's see it."

"Bro, I don't know what you're talking about."

He was much taller than me, and wider than me. As he walked over to me, I was covered by his shadow.

"Come on," he said. "I don't care what you do. I just want to smoke a little. Come on, let me have some."

"I don't got anything."

"You think I'm shocked by a little marijuana? I live in Berkeley where people smoke it on the way to class. Everyday my Lit professor comes to class lit."

"You're just trying to trap me," I said.

"Ah, so you do have some!"

"I didn't say that. But if I did, how would I know you weren't trying to trap me? So you could tell Che I had drugs and then have me sent back."

"For Christ's sake, it's practically legal. There's medicinal marijuana all over California. I predict that someday it will be entirely legal."

"Until that happens, get a prescription."

"You're a little punk," he said, and he gave up, disappointed in me, disappointed that he wasn't going to get any. He looked around the backyard for the part he needed. I could tell he had really wanted some, because he suddenly seemed deflated. His shoulders drooped more than usual. He looked like a sad polar bear.

When he wasn't looking, I pulled the piece of paper out of my sock, unwrapped it and took out the joint. I threw the piece of paper aside.

"Hey, look what I found," I said.

He turned around, still pouting and said, "What?" When he saw the joint he got happy. "I knew it!"

"I just found it," I said. "Just now. Right here on the floor. Maybe the old lady next door has a prescription."

"Light it up," he said, stepping closer.

"*You* light it," I said, and I handed it to him. He took it into his fat fingers. His nails were thick and dirty. He put the joint in his mouth and patted the pockets of his sweatpants looking for a light.

I handed him my lighter. He lit the joint and took a
hit. This wasn't his first time. He took in several tokes,
and held it, his chest expanding. He let out the smoke
and said, "Chronic!"

He handed the joint to me.

"How do you do this?" I asked, looking at it as if it
were a foreign object. "I've never done this before. How
do you do it?"

"Oh, shut up," he said.

"I'll try," I said, "but this is my first time."

※※ ※※ ※※

I was helping Johnny fix a fax machine. "Hand me
that little screwdriver," he said.

"We're out of vodka," I said.

He giggled like a kid.

"Then make it a rusty nail," he said.

I passed him the screwdriver.

"Do you know what an onomatopoeia is?" he asked as
he worked.

"That's a cool word to say," I said, and tried to say it
right, "Onomatopoeia."

"If I may speak onomatopoetically," he said.

"That's even harder to say." I tried it. And then were
both trying to say it, but we couldn't get it right. "I think
I invented a new tongue twister," he said.

"I knew you'd be famous one day."

"An onomatopoeia is a word that makes the sound it
refers to."

"Oh, ok. Yeah! Thanks for explaining that."

"You get it then?"

"I have no idea what you're talking about, onomatopoetically of course."

"It means a word that makes the sound to which it refers, like the word, quack! Quack not only means the sound ducks make, but it also *makes* the sound. Quack! Quack!"

"Okay, I get it," I said. "Like the word smack. If I smack you upside the head, the smack makes a smack?"

"You know, I'm really surprised to find out what a geek you are," he said.

"No, no. That's *Greek*," I said. "My name's Dimitri. Nice to meet you."

"You know what I think my name should be?" he asked. "Had my dear mother a little more foresight than *John*. How original! She completely misnamed me. You know what my name would be?"

"The Comic Book Guy?" I asked.

"Hannibal," he said.

"Like Hannibal Lector?"

"Or Hannibal the Carthaginian."

"Never heard of him. Is he on cable? See, that's why I've never heard of the guy. We only have basic TV."

"Stupid, he's not a Hollywood actor." He looked at me. Saw my face.

"Oh," he said. "You're joking."

"Very good, Johnny-san," I said.

"Hannibal-san" he said. "You know what Hannibal means?"

"What?" I asked.

"Baal is my grace."

"That's kind of creepy that you want to be called a Baal lover. Isn't he like Satan?"

"No, no, he's just a god. In fact, he could be any number of gods."

I recited a passage Jessica had taught me years ago: "I have reserved to myself seven thousand men, who have not bowed the knee to the image of Baal."

"What is that?" he asked.

"My mom used to quote the Bible all the time. She used that one anytime she thought I was worshipping false idols."

"Well, the name can be used for any god, or several gods at once. That's why I like the name because if I can find grace in any number of gods—be my gods money or power or the work I do in life, whatever I make my gods. Because if it refers to *any* god, I can switch 'allegiance' at will and use whatever god I need. I'm protected."

"I don't know, dog. Something doesn't sound right about that."

He held out his arms like a prince, and he proclaimed, "I walk in grace, like the night!"

He held the joint to his lips, but before he took another hit he spoke: "I could step off the sidewalk and cross a city intersection without looking, just walk right through a river of cars—and swoosh!—they'd flow by me like water."

"You're weird," I said.

"Why would I want to be normal? And besides, who decides what's normal? If I were normal, who would I be like? What would normality entail? How come I don't remember voting on its meaning? I would rather not try to live my life according to a mold given to me by the culture, and these days that means popular culture: TV, movies, hip hop music, videogames, iTunes. No, thank you. I would rather create myself *my* way, outside of culture."

"Earth to Johnny! We're losing contact."

He was getting serious, moving his arm back-and-forth. "I will not conform to self images created by popular culture. My worth is *not* in how cool I dress . . . "

"You got that right! People quit wearing sweatpants with elastic at the ankles since before I was born."

"Or how skinny I am."

"Oh, boy! Right again!"

"My worth comes from the gods, that is, the gods *I* choose. The things in life that *I* believe deserve reverence. And you know what that is? Do you know what I revere?"

"Cheeseburgers?" I said.

He giggled and that got me started. I was laughing too. Then he laughed so hard that tears came to his eyes, and he had to bend over. I thought he was coughing and going to die, but he was laughing. That kept me laughing and we were both bent over now laughing like crazy people.

He tried to say something, "That . . . that . . . that . . . " but his laughter wouldn't allow him to speak. It looked like he couldn't even breathe, but he kept trying to say something. "That . . . " and finally it all came out. "That sounds good!"

"What does?"

"Cheeseburgers."

I stood up straight. "No, it doesn't. You know what sounds good?" I said. "Can I draw you?"

"No, think about it!" he said, all excited, like a coach pep-talking his team. "Isn't that the best thing you could ever think of? Come on!"

"What?"

"CHEESEBURGERS! In-N-Out Double Double!"

"Well, no, I could think of something better."

"What could be better?"

"Iliana."

"Who's Iliana?

I wanted to say that she was my girlfriend. "She's a girl who eats the world's best *churros*."

"Oh, *churros!* That sounds great! Almost as good as cheeseburgers. I'm going to make a food run." He walked toward the house.

"No, stop," I shouted like I meant it, like a cop yelling at a criminal.

He turned around. "What is it?"

"Seriously," I said. "I got a better idea. "I'll cook for you."

No one ever cooked in that house. Mostly he went out for fast food: double cheeseburgers with bacon; *carne asada* burritos so fat they looked like babies; a trio of chili cheese dogs with diced onions; and onion rings the size of jailhouse key rings.

Still, they had some items in the kitchen as if someone used to cook, spices, bags of pasta and some frozen meats. I knew I had enough stuff to make a killer spaghetti, so I told Johnny I would cook, but he had his mind set on a Double Double from In-N-Out and a chocolate milkshake.

"Trust me," I said.

I pulled out the ground beef and a can of tomato sauce. I used the gravy from the beef fat and poured it into the sauce. At first it was a bit frustrating not knowing where everything was or if they even had it, a spatula, a wooden spoon, a colander. Anytime I asked Johnny where things were, he said how in the hell would he know and that wasn't part of the deal and if he didn't have food on the table in ten minutes he would go get a Double Double for himself and I could eat the spaghetti alone.

"No-no," I said.

I rushed to cook a meal like a cartoon servant. I made the hurry part of the fun, and *bling!* the Italian chef showed up and he said, "Mama mia! We got-ta no time!"

In twenty minutes, I put before Johnny a bowl of steaming spaghetti topped with red sauce and big cheesy meatballs.

Johnny literally licked his lips as he fell into the chair in front of him, facing the bowl. He didn't touch it, as if waiting for my word before he started. So I sat down opposite him, in front of my bowl, and said "Dig in!"

He went at that food like a starving savage, sauce all over his mouth like blood, dripping onto his T-shirt. He ate and ate, and afterwards he sat back in his chair and said, "That was delicious."

"There's plenty more," I said.

He had another bowl and then a third before I was done with my first. He got a slice of white bread and used it to wipe the sauce from the pan and he ate that too.

"I think I just found a job for you."

And that was how I became my cousin's cook.

I designed a weekly menu, wrote down what I needed and Johnny took me to the market where I picked out vegetables and meat. I convinced him to buy me a better cooking pot, because the one they had was so small I had to cook pasta in shifts. I made him meatloaf and beef stroganoff and *chile verde* burritos with rice and home-made flour tortillas. He let me go online to look up recipes, and I tried stuff I hadn't heard of before chicken Jerusalem, veal saltimbocca, chicken adobo. I was more critical of my work than he was, thinking sometimes the meal was a complete failure, but Johnny would eat up each one as if he hadn't eaten in weeks. When he left the table, he would say, "That was delicious."

When there were leftovers, I put them in the fridge and later the same day I noticed they were gone. Johnny left dirty plates everywhere, and I went around the house collecting them and washing them to keep the kitchen clean and stocked so I could work out of it.

On weekends when Che was home, I cooked for the both of them, eggplant parmesan one night and Chicano spaghetti on the other. She ate her meals with glasses of red wine. After we ate, we all sat at the table talking.

I asked her why she was named La Malinche. Johnny thought I hadn't heard of the legend, so he gave me a lecture about Cortez' Indian translator. She was said to have sold out the indigenous people by helping Cortez subject them. She was Mexico's Benedict Arnold.

Her father was convinced that everyone would betray him. That was why he called her Malinche, his firstborn. He yelled, "La Malinche! You're nothing but a worthless woman. You're a liar."

It was supposed to be an insult, but she came to like the nickname, to call herself that in rebellion. She came to think of her namesake not so much as a betrayer of Mexico, but as an intelligent woman who did what she had to do in order to survive.

"She could speak many languages. Not bad for a girl with no education."

She sipped her wine.

Eventually she started calling herself by the diminutive Che. She said it had double meaning, identification with Malinche as well as the revolutionary Che Guevara.

"My father abandoned everyone," she said. "He was sure they would abandon him, and he treated us like crap. Like we were the enemy. He hit us. He kicked us. Pulled our hair. I did what I needed to survive. I drove the taco truck named 'Tacos Malinche' all the way to Sacramento, where I left it in some parking lot. Then I took a bus to Seattle, and I haven't heard from him since."

I told her I wanted to ask her something about my family.

"I'll do my best," she said.

"Good luck," said Johnny. "She won't even tell me who my father is."

"That's because it's irrelevant," she said.

I asked if she remembered the time my father used to court my mom, going to the taco truck, bringing her flowers, serenading her. "My mom was pretty traditional, I guess."

"I don't know what you're talking about," she said.

"Well, you were at their wedding, weren't you?"

"Wedding? *M'ijo*, your mother went AWOL. She didn't come home one day. I'm not sure that my father ever met Victor."

"What?" I asked, stunned.

She told me that after Jessica "betrayed" my grandfather by leaving the taco truck and staying out all night with some cholo, he never spoke to her again, wanted nothing to do with her. He burned her clothes in the backyard. They were probably living together before they even got married.

My mother had lied to me? Why?

※ ※ ※

Johnny was taking two online architecture classes. He told me that he had decided to make architecture one of his majors. He had three of them: math and engineering were the others.

In one assignment, he had to design an entire office park, complete with fountains and restaurants and parking structures, and he had to do it all within a limited amount of space. He also had to design bridges, not creatively, but mechanically, down to the minute details, with the exact measurements written within the drawing. There was so much work to do for his two online classes that he hardly slept and it put him in a bad mood. He liked smoking weed, because it relaxed him he said. When I ran out, he said "Too bad, so sad," as if it meant nothing to him. But two days later, he asked me if I knew how to get more.

"I'll pay for it," he said.

I didn't know anyone in Modesto. But anyone could figure out how to score, so I had him drive me to a park at the edge of the neighborhood where a lot of cholos hung out. He pulled into the parking lot, his windows rolled up as if he were entering a battle zone. I told him to give me the money. He gave me cash.

"I'll be right back," I said.

"What if you get killed?" he asked.

"Then it's back to fast food for you," I said, opening the door. As soon as it shut, I heard the automatic locks going down.

I recognized the guys right away. You could just tell, because they had clear eyes and strong postures. They were two black guys sitting on a picnic table. They watched me get closer.

"What you want?" one of them said.

I nodded my head, *What's up.*

There was this guy, and he was begging the black guys for something. "Just a little bit," he said.

One of the guys said, "Get out of here, fool."

"Come on, dog, you know I'm good for it."

"Who are you?" one of the guys asked me.

"I'm from Fresno," I said. "Can you hook me up?"

"Of course they can hook you up, man. These guys are the men. They're the ones," said the junkie.

"Hey, shut up," the guy said.

"I'm just saying, you're the man, dog."

He told me to follow him, so I did, and the junkie followed us too. "You better get the out of here," he said, and the junkie stayed behind.

He had the stuff hidden in a hole in the fence. I gave him the money, thanked him.

He said he was there all the time. "Whatever you want."

"This is all I want," I said.

On the way back to the car I could see Johnny watching me, his eyes wide as if he were afraid. The junkie followed me too and asked me what I scored and could he have some. I told him to get lost, but then he started to get all bad-ass on me.

"Who you think you are?" he said, challenging me.

I saw the two guys looking at me and Johnny still looking at me, so when this skinny junkie grabbed my arm, I turned around and pushed him over my outstretched leg and tripped him. As he fell to the ground, the black guys cheered.

When I got back in the car, Johnny was saying, *oh shit oh shit oh shit!*

I threw it at Johnny. "Let's go," I said.

I kept a twenty-dollar broker's fee. He didn't care. He was happy.

One afternoon I had a chicken in the oven and while I was waiting for the food to cook, I sat at the table and sketched a pile of adding machines. I suddenly felt Johnny looking over my shoulders.

"Don't quit your day job," he said.

"I'm just doodling."

"Actually, it's not bad," he said. "You have skills."

He put a book in front of me, opened the page and revealed pencil drawings of boxes. "Do you think you have the skills to reproduce this image?" he said.

"Sure, no problem," I said.

"Can I see?"

"Come back in five minutes," I said. "It's hard to draw when someone's watching."

He went to another part of the house, and I sat and drew box after box after box, an entire mountain of them. I drew monkeys jumping in and out of boxes, children building castles out of boxes, boxes made of metal flying in the air like secret government weapons.

When Johnny came to check my work, he said, "That's not bad. Can I ask you to do something for me?"

He asked me to draw bridges for him, but he wanted me to use a ruler and a pencil and to use the precise measurements he gave me. "It'll really help me out," he said.

I worked all day on his projects, whatever he needed, a perspective on a wall or a staircase. As he looked at my work he whispered, "Not bad."

He wanted a steeple. I drew a steeple. A roof, I drew a roof. A flying buttress, I drew it. I knew he wanted the thing in itself, the technical thing, but sometimes I couldn't help it. When I was drawing the side of a building, I added the shadow that the wall would make, and I drew a broken bottle on the side of the building, so I could play around with light. I put little pieces of light inside the shards of glass. I was eager to show it to Johnny, because I was proud of it.

He shook his head and said, "Yeah, but, I just need the exact proportions I gave you."

I drew streets for him, and windows for him, and bridge after bridge after bridge for him, but never the water flowing underneath or the people walking across for him.

One day I told him I needed a break.

I stayed in my hot, cement room. I pulled out my sketchpad, but I realized that I didn't have any desire to draw. He had ruined it for me. It wasn't fun anymore. I decided to turn on the radio, which was set to some talk radio station. Some woman's voice. *"If you continue to worry about the same things over and over you're probably creating the very situation that you fear."*

I went to the bookshelves in the kitchen and found some poetry books by Neruda and Lorca, bilingual editions, and I sat on the cot and read. I was looking for images to draw, not proportions, not angles, but images that were striking even if they didn't make logical sense. I found one in Neruda I thought I would try:

Y nadie vio la luna que sangraba en mi boca.

And no one saw the moon that was bleeding in my mouth.

I pictured the smile of a woman, her moist red lips, and her teeth white as the bone of the moon, and perched on one of her teeth, I saw a drop of blood.

Suddenly I heard a voice coming from another room. "Who in the hell you think you're talking to?"

It wasn't Johnny's voice.

"I'll knock you out!"

I turned off the radio and listened.

"You think you can treat me like some punk?"

I jumped off the bed and went out into the main part of the house. I saw in the living room that there was some cholo-looking guy in his late twenties. He was a customer, I guessed, and Johnny must have said something smartass. The guy had hold of Johnny's collar and was twisting it, pushing him against the wall. He meant business. Johnny was about to get his butt kicked.

"You think you can treat me like that, huh? I'll mess you up, fat boy."

Johnny was stuttering. "I, I, I meant nothing."

I walked to the edge of the room, my hands by my sides, my fists clenched.

The guy saw me and he loosened his grip on Johnny's collar, but he didn't let go. He looked at me. I mean, he looked hard at me, mad-dogged me, challenged me with his stare.

I stared back.

"You got a problem?" he asked me.

"That's my *primo*," I said.

Slowly, he let Johnny go. He picked up the wireless router Johnny must have sold him and started to walk out. He had to walk right by me. He stopped and looked at me, inches from me. "He's got no respect," the guy said.

"He's like that," I said.

"You should do something about him."

"I'll have a talk with him."

He nodded, as if to acknowledge that things were cool.

I nodded back. The guy left, closing the door quietly behind him.

I looked at Johnny, and I guess I expected him to burst out laughing, maybe wipe sweat off his forehead and say, "That was close," or at the very least, maybe I thought he would say thanks and go back to work and I'd go back to my room and finish drawing the moon bleeding in the mouth of a woman, but that didn't happen.

Johnny broke out in a rage. "You'll have a talk with me?" he yelled.

He started cussing at me, cursing every fricken' cholo that ever lived, and what he did next could only be described as a tantrum, knocking stuff off the table, throwing dishes against the wall.

For the next two weeks, Johnny barely talked to me. I cooked for him but he would go out for fast food and I ended up putting most of what I had cooked into the refrigerator until me or Che ate or it went sour and I had to throw it out. I asked him if he needed any help drawing things for his classes, but he said he was okay, that he'd do it himself. But when he ran out of weed, he asked if I could get him more. As he drove me to the park I said, "Hey, man, I'm sorry if I was out of line. You know, with that guy. I was just acting on instinct. I didn't think about it."

He nodded. He pulled into the park parking lot. "It's all right," he said.

I walked into the park and found the same guy as last time. He recognized me, gave me a handshake—that is, we brushed our fingers together—and then he led me to

the other side of the park, where he had his stuff hidden
in some bushes.

One morning, when I came out of my room for breakfast, Che was sitting at the kitchen table. "Good morning,"
she said. "¿Amaneciste bien?"

"Yes, thank you," I said. "And you?"

"Full of life."

"Cool." I walked over to the refrigerator to take out
some milk. I got the box of cereal and put them on the
table and sat down. Che was eating yogurt and a bran
muffin. She had her laptop open and was viewing some
online newspaper, streaming video clips. I could hear the
president saying something about the economy.

I got a bowl and a spoon and sat down opposite her.
She closed her laptop, shutting down the president's
voice. Now I could hear the faint voices of Johnny's talk
radio show coming from the other part of the house.

She smiled at me. "Victor?" she said.

I poured dry cereal into my bowl. It was Lucky
Charms, and I kept shaking the box, wanting to make
sure that I got plenty of the marshmallow candies, blue
diamonds, green clovers, yellow moons.

I imagined the little leprechaun standing on the table
proudly watching me eat his Lucky Charms, arms akim-
bo. "A fine way to start the day, eh?" he asked me in his
thick, Irish brogue.

"We need to talk, Victor," she said.

"Is everything okay?"

"She wants me Lucky Charms," the Leprechaun said,
sitting on the edge of my bowl.

"Would you like to go home?"

"Really?"

"I think you're ready. You're a good boy, and that's what I told your mom. I told her that your energy was just a bit unfocused, but that you're a good kid. Now, listen: You need to keep up the Productive Activity, and you want to put that into your school work. You need to get more involved. Join the debate team. You need to make school your focus of energy. I promise, Victor, you'll do all right. You got enough time to make high school mean anything you want it to mean. That's a gift, Victor. Do something with it. Use it as a tool to get whatever it is you want in life."

After breakfast, I happily packed my bags, shoving in my clothes as if they were dirty laundry. Quark stood out in the back patio looking in at me, waving goodbye.

"I'm going home!" I said.

"I know," she said sniffling sadly.

The leprechaun appeared next to her, a few feet shorter than her. "I'll keep your friend company, I will," he said.

They stood side-by-side, waving goodbye to me.

Jessica didn't say much on the way home from the bus station. She smelled like perfume and wore a lot of lipstick and eye shadow. Maybe I had just forgotten what it was like being around her. She had so much hair, and she dressed nice, too. She wore high-heeled shoes. As she drove, she was chewing gum, Wrigley's Spearmint. It was such a familiar smell it kind of made me sentimental about being home.

"Can I have a stick of gum?" I asked.

She took her big purse—which separated us in the front seat—put it on her lap and felt around inside. She shook her head, as if she couldn't get over some idea that bothered her. I figured it had to do with me, so I kept shut. I looked out my window and saw that we were passing an inner-city ballpark. The diamond was empty but there were a few teenagers hanging out against the backstop.

I turned around and saw that Jessica had the stick of gum in her hand and was holding it out to me. I grabbed it.

She shook her head again, amazed at some thought she had.

"What is it?" I said.

"I don't know how you did it."

"Did what?"

"Convince your aunt that you're not a troublemaker."

"What are you talking about?"

"He's a good kid. He's not a gang member," she quoted her sister.

Jessica suddenly shifted into a serious, firm voice. "I saw it, Victor, with my own eyes. You brought drugs and weapons into my house! You sneak out all the time even though I expressly forbid it. *Tengo ojos*, you know. Believe me, this summer was very peaceful without you."

"Thanks," I said. "That's very motherly of you to say."

"I don't know how you did it, but you charmed her into thinking you're this great guy or something. I thought she was smarter than you, but you tricked her. Well, I'm through with you. I don't care anymore what kind of life you lead, but you bring none of it into my house. You can eat there, you can sleep there, but you do not live your lifestyle there."

"What *lifestyle?*"

"Oh, shut up," she said. "You know damn well what I'm talking about. And none of your friends are welcome in the house. Not even Harold. I'm making both of us free. How does that sound?"

"What?"

"I'm free from worrying about you. You're free from—how do they say?—your mother's G-string."

"What?"

"I'm not going to try and control you anymore."

"*Apron* strings. I'm free from your *apron* strings."

"You do whatever you want."

"I did what *you* wanted. I went to stay with Che and Johnny the entire summer, and you know what? They liked me. It was nice."

"Why don't you go live with them forever?"

Sometimes, she would come home late, around about midnight, and you could tell she had had a few drinks, because they made her cheeks red. Sometimes, late at night, when she was in bed and the lights were out in her room, she'd be talking with someone on her cell phone. She laughed a lot.

So now I had complete freedom. I could do anything I wanted to.

Even though I was three months late, one of the first things I did was go to the Cherry Auction to find Iliana.

There were two parts of the flea market, the old and the new. In the new section they sold new things: clothes, baseball caps and T-shirts, CDs, boom boxes with a bunch of flashing lights.

Then there was the old section, where people spread their stuff out on tables or on the ground on blankets, and they tried to get what they could for dishes, clocks, yellowing stuffed animals. I liked going through the boxes of books, but most of them were Bibles, the hardcover kind the Gideons left in motel rooms. And there were out-of-date textbooks, history books and math books. I found myself looking through an old, math book called *Introduction to Calculus.* I read the passages students had underlined and the comments they wrote in the margins. I skimmed the pages of history books and read dog-eared passages highlighted in yellow. In one book I found a note someone had written years earlier, a telephone number and the words *Please call me* with two exclamation points.

"Fifty cents," the woman said. She walked closer to me, on the opposite side of the table, and she stared to arrange things. She was Vietnamese.

"Did you say something?" I asked.

"One dollar. Good price."

"Uh, thanks," I said.

"That's an old book," she said. "Very valuable."

I put it back down.

"Okay, fine! Fifty cents," she said. "You're good at this!" she said, pointing to me, as if conceding defeat. She drew a plastic bag from her pocket and whipped it in the air so it snapped and puffed up, and then she began to put the book inside. "You will love it!"

"No, no thank you," I said. And I walked off.

"Make me an offer!"

I walked down more aisles, past more tables and blankets of old stuff, radios, VCRs and DVD players, lighting fixtures and plumbing parts, tools and boxes of used clothes, and then I went to the *churro* booth, but she never came.

✿❧ ✿❧ ✿❧

One day, I was hanging out with some friends, Equis and a guy named José. We were just standing around on the freeway overpass watching the cars slide by.

We were talking about what kind of car we would want, and José was trying to describe a car whose name he couldn't remember. He snapped his fingers three times, as if that would give him the answer.

He kept saying, "You know what I mean? You know, that car from Germany but its real nice and it's not a Mercedes!"

I knew what he was talking about, so I pulled a pencil out of my school backpack and opened a notepad.

I drew the BMW.

"Does it looks like this?" I said.

They watched as I drew it.

"*¡Qué suave!*" José said, looking at the car. "How did you do that?"

"It's easy," I said. "It's just line and curve."

"Can you draw an Escalade?" Equis asked.

I closed my eyes and looked into my mind at the Escalade within it. I saw one all blinged out, a sunroof, gold bumper and rims. Then I opened my eyes and reproduced the angles and curves and lines that made the shape. I showed it to the guys.

"That's my ride!" said Equis.

"But that's not the kind of car you're going to drive, Equis," I said. "You're going to drive something like this." I closed my eyes and pictured a beat-up Ford Taurus, and I reduced it to curve and line. Then I opened my eyes and drew it. José laughed and Equis said, "Aw, that's messed up!"

"I'm just messing with you. This is what I'll drive."

This time I knew I didn't have to close my eyes to deconstruct the image into forms, I just drew it. A big, mean limousine with tinted windows, and I slid the pad to the gaze of my friends.

"I won't even have to drive. Someone will do it for me."

"Hell yeah!" Equis said.

"Damn," José said.

"What about a *ruca*?" asked Equis. "Got to have a *ruca* with a ride like that."

In my mind I saw a girl, a cartoonish, lowrider babe in short shorts and a tight shirt.

Suddenly an image of a real girl flashed in my mind: Iliana. When that image transposed over the cartoon image, it didn't fit. It wasn't right. I felt this emptiness—real quick—because I knew that I couldn't draw her. I realized I couldn't draw people, only cartoon people. When it came to representations of real people with real souls, I couldn't get it right.

I tried to draw a girl, but she came out as a cartoon with exaggerated womanly curves.

"Well," I said, showing them the drawing, "in real life she's a lot better than this."

Something disturbed me about the image, because it was false, so phony that it made me nauseated. It felt like lying.

After that day I became obsessed with drawing people, because I wanted to feel something. Then one day, it happened.

I was sitting at the Cherry Auction when I started drawing a woman standing in line at the *churro* stand. It was cool that day, and she had a scarf wrapped around her. I continued to draw her, even after she had left. Suddenly the woman on my sketchpad became real. I drew a ponytail and gave her a birthmark on her upper lip. She wasn't a cartoon, she was a drawing. It felt good. It felt like I was releasing a soul. She was a real soul that was released into my drawing, a real angel from the head of my pen.

I started drawing all kinds of people, everywhere I went: kids playing in the street, old people sitting on the bus, Jessica at the kitchen table doing the books for the restaurant.

Then I started painting. The art room at school had free hours when you could come in and use their stuff. I started painting in acrylics. At first, I was doing trite Chicano images. I drew sexy Aztec women in the arms of Aztec men. I painted lowriders and buxom Chicanas standing next to the cars with short shorts, but I knew the paintings had no energy behind the image. They were lies, they were superficial, but my friends loved them and hung them on their walls. "You should sell your art at the flea market," Equis said.

At night, I would close my eyes in bed and picture myself drawing faces, picture someone *being* drawn. One night I dreamed I was standing on the shores of a lake. It was a sunny day, and I saw the water ripple like shards of a mirror, and in each shard I saw a face, thousands of faces reaching to the horizon of the lake, all of them looking at me, floating on the lake, waiting for me to draw them, to release their souls.

Then I started to draw things that were hard to draw, a face looking in a mirror, school children running to catch a bus, a car accident on a busy intersection.

My skill became a game for my friends and me.

We were sitting around the benches in the schoolyard when José said, "Man, I sure could use a taco." I opened my sketchpad and drew him a taco dripping with meat and cheese.

He looked at it and said, "Where's the onions?"

I drew an onion and a knife and a cutting board and slid the pad over to him and said, "Cut them yourself."

"I need a *cuete*," said Equis.

I drew a handgun, a six shooter.

"No, *vato*, I want a Glock."

I drew a bow and arrow.

"Aw, that's messed up."

"Man, I sure wish we could take a road trip to the beach today," José said, and I drew him an ocean. "With girls," he said, and I drew girls playing volleyball on the beach.

We found out that this was a great way to meet girls. We'd be hanging out at the benches at school and Equis would say to a girl, "Hey, my friend and I can give you anything you want. Go ahead, name something you've always wanted but can't afford. We'll get it for you."

One girl said, "I want a nice house by Woodward Park," and I drew her one.

Another told us that she wanted money. She looked at her girlfriends and laughed.

I drew a box overflowing with money, $100-bills falling out.

The girl laughed at it, and one of her friends asked to go next.

A car.

A house.

New shoes.

A stereo with big speakers.

A new dress hanging in an empty closet.

Then one Sunday afternoon, José, Equis and I were hanging out at the Cherry Auction, when I saw this dark-skinned Chicana walk by.

Iliana.

My heart beat hard.

She was wearing white pants which made her skin look darker.

I told the guys I wanted to meet her.

"Meet who?" Equis asked.

I pointed to her. She was walking past the booths and through the crowd.

She swerved in and out of people like a panther.

"Ask her what she wants," I told them. "I want to draw for her."

We followed her through the market. She stopped at the *churro* booth and waited in line. Equis walked up to her all cool-like, like he wanted to pick her up.

She wore a red tank top. He tapped her on the shoulder, and she turned around.

"My homeboy and I are like magic and shit," he said. "We can get you anything you want—poof!—just like that. Go ahead, tell us what you want, anything in the world, and we'll make it appear before your eyes."

That was when she noticed me. She didn't look too excited like I had wanted her to be. I wanted her to put her hands over her mouth and scream with delight and then run into my arms for a hug, but she just stood there as if running into me meant nothing. That made me feel a little bad, a little defensive. I figured that she hadn't been thinking about me in the same way.

"So what you do want?" Equis asked.

"Peace on Earth," she said, looking in my eyes.

"Naw, that's not what we mean," Equis said. "We mean anything *real*, you know? Something real."

"How come peace can't be real?" she asked.

"Choose a *thing*," he said.

"No, no," I said. "She wants peace on earth, I'll give her peace."

I started to move my pen. The drawing turned out to be—and I have no idea why, because I drew guided only by the rhythm of the pen—an image of an open umbrella in the rain, underneath which was a couple, a man and a woman walking together across a freeway overpass. They were pressed so close side-by-side that their silhouettes (which I shaded with the pen) looked like one body, yet you could tell they were two. Their faces looked real. Behind them, I put trees and rooftops of the city. I wanted to create a feeling, but I couldn't keep Iliana waiting for too long, so I used simple lines and made elbows like the letter L upside down and inside them I put tiny dots of ink. In the context of the image-as-a-whole, the upside-down Ls became buildings with windows. I had never done this before.

As I drew, I felt so intensely wonderful that the emotion found a way to seep from my interiors and buzzed on my arms and went into the drawing. When I finished, I looked up and saw Iliana standing there. I handed it to her.

I wanted her to look at the image for a long time, and she looked at it for a long time. Her toes were pointed in.

"Can I keep it?"

Equis tried to act all player on her.

"What you gonna give *me*, baby?" he said, looking her up and down, stepping closer to her, but she was still looking at me.

Iliana was moving up in the *churro* line.

"I told you they were the world's best *churros*," she said. "Want one?"

"Yeah, sure," I said.

I told Equis I would catch up with him a little later on. He was a little pissed off, but he left.

I stood in line with Iliana. We didn't say anything. We just stood there next to each other.

Finally she said something. "Is that how you pick up girls?"

"Pretty cool trick, huh?"

"Your friend's a wannabe player."

"He's all right."

"So how long has it been?" she asked. "Victor, if I remember correctly."

I wanted to say *Too long*, but that would have sounded too corny, or like I was trying too hard to play her. "A couple of months," I said.

"You didn't show up," she said.

"Well you said to meet you on any Saturday."

"No, I said on Saturday, I think it was implied I meant *that* Saturday."

Iliana reached the front of the line and asked for two *churros*. She handed a few dollars to the vendor and turned around. She handed me a *churro*. I nodded *thanks*. We walked into the crowd. She took a bite and for a second, closed her eyes and chewed, as if the flavor was that good.

I took a bite. "Wow. You're right," I said.

"Good *churros*, huh?" she said, chewing.

"Worth the wait," I said, chewing. When I finished chewing that mouthful, I said, "Some things are worth waiting for, don't you think?"

She rolled her eyes.

"What?"

"That's really corny."

We took another bite almost at the same time and we chewed.

We nodded our heads, as if to say, yes, yes, it was delicious.

🌸 🌸 🌸

When I got to the apartment, Jessica was sitting on the table, a Diet Pepsi in front of her, her hands folded. She gave me that look, like I was in trouble, and she told me to sit down.

I sat opposite her. "What is it now?"

"I have something to tell you, Victor."

"Yeah, that's pretty obvious," I said.

She sighed deeply. "You're so sarcastic," she said. "You always think everyone's dumber than you. You're father was like that. You're just like him, you know."

"Sorry," I said. "You liked Dad, didn't you?"

"Of course I did. He was my husband. You're not. Anyway, I have big news."

"I'm ready."

"I'm getting married."

"What?"

"There's going to be a lot of changes."

"You're getting married? Who? Why?"

"I waited long enough, Victor. I waited many, many years."

"I didn't know you were waiting."

"That's not what I mean. I mean, it is not disrespectful to your father for me to marry again. Read the Bible."

"Who are you marrying?"

"Mr. Chávez."

"The owner of the Taco Palace #3? He's like 100 years old!"

"He's not that old. He's a good man. He worked hard all his life and made something for himself. He has a house, he owns an apartment building and makes money just collecting the rent. Everything he has will belong to me now too. His daughters *se ponen locas, pero ni modo.* He wants me as his wife, and I said yes. We're going to sign an agreement."

"What are the terms of this agreement?"

"That doesn't matter. What matters is that this makes me the owner too."

She looked around the apartment as if she were seeing something about herself she didn't like. "We're moving out of this place. We're moving into his house," she said. "You'll have your own room. He has a big backyard. You'll like it there."

"But . . ."

"Victor, you want to hear something good? You know what this means for you? You can someday manage a Taco Palace, maybe all of them. I'll teach you everything I know. You can have a career!"

"I'm not sure the restaurant business is what I'm interested in. I think I want to be an artist."

"Oh, I'm not talking hobbies. You can do whatever you want on your free time, I'm talking about a real career. You're a great cook, *m'ijo.* One of the best I know. I can't tell you how I love to watch you cook, adding this spice or that one, tasting your sauces with a wooden spoon. You're good at it. You have talent. For now you learn the business, but in a few years, who knows, maybe you can open your own restaurant, gourmet food and everything.

You can call it whatever you want. Victor's Place. *M'ijo,* don't you see what a great opportunity this is for us?"

"But at what price?"

"What do you mean by that?"

"Do you love him?"

"Don't be so one-sided. If you don't want to come, that's all right with me. Live in the street if you want."

"It's not that. It's just . . . Give me some time to get used to this."

"I got to go," she said. "He's taking me to dinner tonight somewhere nice. Start packing, okay?"

"Packing? Mom, this is too weird."

"I like when you call me mom. You should always call me that." She touched my cheek, gently, and she looked at me with soft eyes. "I won't love you any less," she said. *"Te lo juro."*

"I'm not really . . . "

I was going to say that I wasn't concerned about how much she loved me, but I knew she would have taken it wrong. "You'll see," she said. "Things are going to be better than ever."

She grabbed her purse and turned to leave the apartment. She walked across the room, without saying a word, her heels tapping on the hard floors.

PART THREE
THE STRAVINSKY RIOTS

My girlfriend was a genius. I don't mean that she was *real* smart. I mean she was a certified genius. She joined a club for geniuses called MENSA, and they even gave her a T-shirt with that name written across the front. I teased her about it, because in Spanish *mensa* meant a dumb girl.

We were both seniors in high school, but she liked going to Fresno State to study and use the library. One day we were sitting under this giant tree, which gave us a spot of shade. The day was beautiful. She was reading, and she had books and papers spread around her and an open laptop. She wore her glasses, her hair tied up, looking all student-like. She was reading some thick book that looked as old as time, and she was so absorbed that she hunched over it, as if an invisible energy was pulling her into the pages. I was sketching her, but I started to feel like she was too good for me, that she deserved someone better than me. I never admitted it to her, but I was afraid I would lose her.

Suddenly, I felt something tickling my back, inside my shirt.

I stood up.

I wanted to believe it was a leaf that fell from the tree and floated down into the back of my shirt. I was about to take it out, but whatever it was suddenly crawled up my spine. Then it crawled down again. I could feel little legs twittering across my flesh.

"Damn!" I yelled, trying to catch it or squash it. I probably looked like a crazy dog trying to catch its tail.

"Are you all right?" she asked.

"There's a spider on my back!" I said. I took off my shirt and waved it around like a bullfighter.

She stayed calm, slowly taking off her glasses. "Hmm," she said, closing her eyes, as if to think about it. She opened them again and put her glasses back on. "Victor, do you know what?"

I was too busy panicking to answer her.

"I'm reading about solipsism," she said. "Do you know what that is?"

"I'm dealing with a deadly spider," I said, examining every inch of fabric. I was shirtless, and she used to tell me she liked how I looked without a shirt, like a Mayan warrior. I wondered if she was watching me, enjoying the show.

"It means everything in the world exists only in our own mind. We create reality. Isn't that a cool idea? We confuse our perceptions with reality, but the word we give to reality *is* perception. Each of us has a different reality! Isn't that a cool idea?"

"Hey, *mensa*," I said. "I'm being eaten by a tarantula!"

"You're fine," she said. "It's your perception."

I didn't find a spider, or anything else.

"You created the tarantula," she said.

"It was probably a bead of sweat," I said, putting on my shirt and buttoning it up one by one, trying to look like a sexy Mayan warrior.

She knew what I was doing and rolled her eyes.

"Is it working?" I asked.

"Yeah, it kind of is," she said. We started making out.

She called herself a Chicana because she thought the word Hispanic was too general. "*Somos cubanos, mexicanos, chicanos. ¡Feministas!* But what does Hispanic even mean? I never met anyone from Hispania."

One day, she cut off most of her hair. She said she liked it short, because it was less hassle. I loved her long, silky hair, and I was disappointed. But when I told her that, she got angry and told me that I had to learn to separate my *image* of her from the real her. "Long hair is a male construct of feminine beauty."

I loved the disorganized pile of books in her bedroom, the way she would be in anyone's face if they tried to treat us unfairly. I loved the tattoo of the half moon she put above her right hipbone. I loved how she got into intense political discussions with her mom and dad. I would sit there and watch them, not saying anything, amazed that a family could be that way with each other. They'd talk around the table, her parents smoking, drinking, until late hours of the night, and they all moved effortlessly from English to Spanish. Iliana loved to argue during those family discussions. With her short hair, there was something edgy about her beauty. She was all angles, shoulders, long arms, sharp elbows.

For fun she read Michio Kaku's *Parallel Universes*, which was something her friends at school were doing. They were into parallel universes and wormholes and quantum weirdness. She liked to imagine time travel.

"If we found a wormhole," she told me, as we were walking into the library at Fresno State, books and statues rising around us. "We could time travel. If the laws of physics say it's possible, then it must be inevitable."

"Why does that make it inevitable?" I asked, like I wanted to argue with her.

"What in the universe is possible that hasn't happened at least once?"

I grabbed her hand and led her into the stacks of books. "We haven't made out in the library." I pulled her closer to me, kissed her neck, but she pushed me away.

"That is so inappropriate," she said, walking away.

"It is?" I asked, following her. "Why?"

"I'm not a toy that can be played with at your whim."

"I didn't mean it like that."

She stopped walking, turned around and faced me. She kissed me on the cheek. "I know," she said. "But think about it: I'm having a conversation about a subject that intrigues me and you completely negate it by turning me into an object of sexuality."

"Sorry," I said.

"I bet you're disappointed I don't wear short skirts and high heels."

"You would look great!" I said.

She slapped me on the chest and turned around and kept walking. "You're a great guy, but you can still go either way."

"Either way?"

"In a parallel universe, you're a macho, gang-banging misogynist. Just like your friend Equis."

"I am not!" I said, telling myself to look up the word misogynist. I didn't know what it was, but it didn't sound good.

We went to different schools. Hers was one of those satellite schools where they bussed brilliant kids from all over the city so they could be together. My school was the biggest joke in the county. It wasn't in the city limits, even though it was urban. There were a lot of gang members, a lot of fighting, and over fifty percent of my class wouldn't graduate.

The summer before I died, my grades were bad, because I didn't care about school. I just wanted to hang out with friends, meet girls, draw cartoons. But after my summer with Che, I started doing well. I quickly became an honors student. I liked to read, and that made the teachers think I was smart.

Now I took advanced placement classes. I liked it when I was the smartest kid in the class. I wanted my papers to be better than the others, wanted to know more than the others knew. I wanted to keep up with my girl-friend.

Jessica and I lived with the old man. At first, I thought we would be living in a mansion, but his house was in the same barrio as ours, about a mile away from our apartments. He had a bigger house than most of the neighborhood, a tall fence that surrounded it, and these stupid looking fountains with statues in the front yard. We had ceramic lions at the entrance of the driveway.

His name was Ernie Chávez. He was more Chicano than Mexican. His Spanish wasn't that good.

After my mom took over the business, he retired and spent most of his time at home watching TV or at local bars drinking with his buddies. Jessica didn't care what he did, except for one thing. He spent a lot of time at the Indian Casino outside of town gambling his money, so Jessica restricted how much money he could have access to at one time. She set up a bank account for him, which she called his gambling funds.

One time he had some of his old men friends over the house. They busted out with beer and music, playing all those old-School, rock bands like War, El Chicano and Santana. It was kind of funny to see, especially when one of the old *vatos* pulled out a *leño* and passed it around.

Ernie didn't try to be my father. I'd be turning eighteen soon, and maybe he hoped I'd be out of there. I didn't like him or dislike him. He was just there, and that was all right for both of us.

I worked with Jessica ten hours a week as a line cook. I made tacos and enchiladas according to the exact specs, and I was never able to do anything creative or even slightly gourmet.

Working in one of her restaurants, I got to know what she was like. I understood now why the old man had relied on her when she was a manager. She ran those restaurants like a general. Employees were afraid of her. Some of them tried to make friends with me because they knew I was her son. She dealt with them professionally, all business, no smiles, no personal questions. She was the boss.

She opened a restaurant on the north side of town, in a neighborhood where rich people lived. The original Taco Palace had become so popular that people had been driving all the way to the barrio just to eat there, and there were lines out the door. She called it Taco Palace #4, but I told her that she should have a more creative name, something like "The Screaming Aztec." I even offered to paint the sign. She said that I didn't know a thing about business.

She got rid of her old car and bought a fancy SUV luxury model, a Mercedes, with an onboard computer and a bunch of flashing lights.

I set up a little area in the backyard where I painted, behind sheets on a clothesline which seemed like walls. I couldn't paint in the house because the smell bothered everyone, and the garage didn't have enough windows to be a studio. You needed a lot of light to paint.

I would spend hours in our yard painting. I did all kinds of barrio images, lowriders, clowns, the tragedy and comedy masks, and I sold them to friends.

The summer before my senior year, I was able to buy a car. It wasn't fancy, but it got me places. I could pick up Iliana.

I had spending money now, and I even started to make extra money selling stuff to my friends, although that wasn't why I did it. Still, the extra money was there.

After I sold a bag to some kid, I kept telling myself, *I'm not a drug dealer.*

❃❃ ❃❃ ❃❃

The Honors Humanities teacher, Mr. García, pulled a CD player from the classroom closet. It was one of those old systems people used to call ghetto blasters. As he plugged it in, he told us that the music he was about to play, *The Rite of Spring* by Igor Stravinsky, was so unlike anything ever heard and that it had caused a riot in the concert hall.

"Bunch of crap," I said from the back of the room.

He was kind of geeky. He looked up, adjusted his glasses, looked around and said, "Pardon?"

"How could music cause a riot?"

"Exactly," he said. "How could a work of art cause riots? Isn't that astounding? Think of it! Music so different from what people wanted and expected that it caused a riot."

He held a CD case that said *The Rite of Spring.*

"Upon hearing this music," he said, "people threw rocks, smashed each other's heads with chairs. It was an all-out riot."

"Like the Rodney King riots?" asked a boy.

He opened the CD case and pulled out the disk. "I suppose so," he said.

I sat forward at my desk, ready to hear music so powerful that it caused violence.

He wrote on the chalkboard:

Igor Stravinsky 1882-1971.

The music started, violent and wicked, like wails and screeches, like symphonic Death. It was like the clatter of metal. But then it got uniform, like marching soldiers coming to pillage a town. As I listened to it, I fell more and more into the landscape of the music. I knew which side I would have taken in the riots.

I hated everything I had ever painted, ever. I had never even tried to paint anything that would cause a riot.

When the music was over, Mr. García stood silent for a while. He had his eyes closed. The window frame shined behind him, and he looked like a monk after worship. He ejected the CD, lifted it out by the edges, and put it back into the case.

That was when I looked out the window and saw the cholo tree.

It was an almond tree with two main branches reaching into the sky like arms with muscles, so it looked like a man reaching for the sun.

Chicano students had carved their initials onto the chest and biceps of the tree, things I had seen before: *Beto con Alma, La Sleepy. Equis con safos y qué,* carved hearts, crosses.

The tree was a cholo with prison tattoos on his arms and chest.

I wanted to paint it.

I would put vague shapes hovering around the tree, dark energy, blurs of blue, blurs of gray, blurs of red, and they would be cholo spirits, a bunch of them surrounding the tree. They died in drive-bys or fights, and all of them had been raging from the dead for so long that their anger became energy so dark it swirled around the foot of the tree.

That would make a great painting! I thought.

I recalled something about my death. I remembered seeing shapes shooting in and out of light, maybe human shapes.

Iliana had once told me that she refused to study for her chemistry midterm because all it consisted of was memorization of the periodic chart. "It's irrelevant," she had said. "The teacher and the book claim that the 100 atoms that make up the chart are what the entire universe is composed of. The WMAP satellite disproved that, like, ages ago. I want to study what the universe *is* made of."

"And what is that?"

"Twenty-three percent of the universe is made up of dark matter. Seventy-three percent is made up of dark energy."

"What are they?"

"Dark matter and dark energy?"

"Yeah? What are they?" I asked.

"Nobody knows," she said, "but wouldn't a more appropriate test be to speculate on what it *could* be? I'm supposed to be in an honor's program, right? And they're having us memorize numbers and letters?"

Somehow *dark matter* and *dark energy* made sense to me.

After my death, my body sometimes would freeze, and I would start shaking and I thought I was dying again. I saw my dad standing in the light. My body was made of dark matter and I felt myself spinning, and then I passed out.

One time I woke up at a stoplight, a left-turn lane, the arrow green and cars behind me honking their horns. It only happened twice, but that was enough to scare me that it might happen again.

※ ※ ※

The dead cholos floated around the tree like mist on a cold day.

I pulled out my sketchpad, and as Mr. García spoke about the Stravinsky riots, I started with the tree itself.

I drew it in pencil.

I tried to make it look like both tree and cholo. I wanted to paint a tree that had lived a hard life, crying now, paying for *la vida loca* he had led as a young tree.

I drew as if in a trance, the pencil swishing across the page, my body evaporating into dark energy and vibrating the pencil.

I drew mist around the foot of the tree.

"Victor?" Mr. García asked, concerned, as if trying to pull me back to reality.

"What?" I asked. I looked up. I was dizzy.

"Are you all right?" he asked. He leaned into me. "Are you on something?"

"Just drawing," I said.

He looked at the drawing on my desk. "You drew that? How's that possible?"

I looked down on my pad and couldn't believe what I saw. The drawing I had done in a trance was wicked-looking, like the landscape of hell, a barren desert at night. I had shaded everything so the entire page was part of the mood, a moon barely visible through the clouds. It was night. It was foggy, and there was a tree on a hill. It looked like a cholo. It was the best drawing I had ever done, somehow. I didn't feel like I had done it. It was dark energy flowing through me.

❧ ❧ ❧

One day Mr. García announced a special treat. After working hard to convince a lot of school officials to give him money, he was going to take his Honors class on a field trip to San Francisco. We would visit the museums and see the paintings in real life instead of on a screen, like we usually did. He said that for the first time, for most of us, we would be able to see the works of Van Gogh, Picasso, Rembrandt, the sculptures of Rodin and Camille. "This trip will be all day long," he said, "so pack your lunch and dinner or bring some money to buy your meals over there."

He handed us permission slips to be signed by our parents. He looked happy passing them out, like he was giving out green cards or something.

"They have some of the world's greatest works of art," he said. "I love that city. Do you know I spend my summers there? I need to get out of Fresno."

He stopped passing out the slips and stood up straight. "Oh, gracious!" he said. "The first time I saw a Van Gogh up close and personal, Oh! Tears came to my eyes. Literally."

For some reason, I thought of Equis. We hadn't seen each other for about a year. Jessica had told me that he had left his mom's house and was in a gang, but of course she thought everyone was in a gang.

Mr. García continued. "I spend my Spring Breaks over there, too. Oh, if only I could live there year round. I wouldn't say that San Francisco has anything comparable to the Louvre, but they have some amazing collections."

"What's the Loo-ver?" I asked.

"Oh! It's the most beautiful museum in the world."

After class, he asked how my painting was going. I was working with oil paints, which were hard for me to get used to. There were a lot of things that were hard to get right in the painting, like the mist around the tree. It looked like snow, or giant cotton balls.

"No matter what I do, when I paint, everything looks like a cartoon," I said.

"What's wrong with that?"

"I want my paintings to be a little more serious," I said.

"Well, maybe you're being too hard on yourself."

"Cartoons don't start riots."

"Maybe you should take a painting class," he said.

"They don't have one here."

"I could teach you a few techniques. I used to be a painter, you know. I know some things."

"Do you still paint?

"Who has time?" Then he leaned over and whispered into my ear. "Victor, if you *really* want to be an artist, you should go to Paris."

"All right. I'll leave tomorrow."

"The world's best artists go there."

"The best artists in Aztlán don't go there," I said.

"What is Azz Lawn?"

"It's the Chicano homeland," I said.

"Oh, Chicano," he said, waving the word off with his hands. "I hate that word."

"Is that why you don't use Chicano literature in this class?" I asked. "You use all those dead white people."

"I don't choose books because of the ethnicity of the writer. I think Sandra Cisneros is a fine writer, but her work doesn't fit into the scope of the class. And those other Chicano novels, well, I refuse to use any novel that glorifies gangs and life in the barrio. Quite frankly, I'm tired of reading about cholos.

"Here's my unsolicited advice," he said. "I think you could be a great artist."

"A Chicano artist," I said.

"But I hope you become more than that."

I picked up Iliana in front of her school where she stood waiting on the sidewalk talking to her friends, two white kids, a boy and a girl. They looked sort of geeky cool, like journalism students, the kind of kids that young adult novels are written about. As I watched her talking to them, before she saw me, I realized that she was a geek too, just like them, only with dark skin. Her short hair looked all spiky, like that of a retro 1980s girl rocker, and she wore a jean skirt and a tank top with the Apple logo across the chest. She spent most of her day with these kids, and some nights too, when they studied together. Sometimes when they had an out-of-town debate, they even spent weekends together in hotels with the debate coach.

Now they were talking and laughing. The girl with her had stringy, blonde hair and glasses. I got out of the car, and the boy saw me. He had red hair and freckles. He must have recognized me from before, because he told Iliana to turn around and *look who's here* (I could read his lips). She did turn around. Maybe she wasn't sure what he wanted her to see, and maybe she had forgotten I would be picking her up. She looked right through me, right past me. I was invisible to her. If solipsism were true and we created our own reality, she created one without me in it.

I had to wave my arms a few times to get her attention, and even when she saw me completely framed in
her vision, she seemed not to recognize me—for a flash.
Finally her brain must have told her who she was looking
at, and only then did she get excited to see me. But right
between the times that she recognized me and the excited look on her face—for less than a second—another look
flashed across her eyes, one that seemed to me like
shock, as if she had forgotten she had a boyfriend like
me. I still dressed like a cholo, I guess.

I had baggy pants, a big Oakland Raiders T-shirt, and
as I stood there, students looked my way as if wondering
if I would I start trouble. The campus cops were looking
my way, watching me with their arms crossed.

Why did I dress like a cholo?

I had never felt so ridiculous in my life, as if my baggy
pants were clown clothes. Iliana said goodbye to her
friends—hugging both the boy with the red hair and the
girl with glasses—and she walked over to me, her face
now smooth and in love.

I held her in my arms and she felt good.

I took in her smell.

"Victor," she said. "I forgot you were picking me up
today."

"Do you have other plans?"'

"No, of course not. I'm just happy you're here."

I kissed her on the neck.

"How would you like to go to San Francisco?" I asked
her.

"The church? The city?"

I told her about the field trip, but I said that we could
drive over there ourselves. The class was going to drive
into the city, spend the day there, drive back and get

home at night. I figured I would just take my own car, meet the class there, and that way Iliana and I could spend the weekend there.

"Where would we stay?" she asked.

"A hotel, I guess."

"Can we do that?"

"Why not?" I asked.

"Don't you have to be eighteen? Don't we have to have adult supervision?"

"Really, *mensa*? You think we'll need supervision? I think we'll be fine in a hotel together."

"I bet we would be. And do me a favor, *mi amor*?"

"What is it?"

"Don't call me *mensa*, please. I don't like it."

❋ ❋ ❋

I got paid that week. When I picked up my check, I thought about getting a gift for Iliana. I went to the mall to get her a stuffed dog or a box of candies, something traditional and old-fashioned like that. But then I remembered that she wasn't traditional or old-fashioned. So maybe I would get her a book of poems by Sor Juana Inés de la Cruz, or a candle to burn in her bedroom, something that released a scent that she would smell while she was laying on her bed, cinnamon, jasmine, patchouli oil. I wanted to get her something that would make her smile.

I went inside the mall.

I looked at perfumes, stuffed animals, bins of colorful candy, gumdrops and suckers and bonbons. I stopped in front of Victoria's Secret, imagining myself buying her something sexy, but I knew she would get pissed off at me for objectifying her.

I looked at books and CDs and coffee mugs and pens and earphones, but somehow I found myself in the Gap looking through a rack of pants, not for women, but for men. I always thought The Gap was where white people shopped. I usually got all my clothes at places like Sears or the flea market, but here I was in the Gap, where everything was hip and brightly colored and young people who looked like characters from a TV show were giggling with each other as they looked at stuff.

One of the girls who worked there came up to me, at first reluctantly, as if she were asked to touch a deadly snake. She came closer and then stood there about to say something to me, like maybe *Get out of the store.* She was college-age with sunken cheeks like a runway model, and had thin brown hair. She might have been Latina or Asian, you couldn't tell, but she was kind of light-skinned, and her eyes were light brown. She looked me up and down, as if to say, *Oh, my God!*

I thought she was about to turn around and leave me alone, but she said, "Can I help you?"

"I guess I want a new look," I said.

That seemed to make her pretty happy. "Let's have some fun!" she said.

She pulled a bunch of pants from the shelves, some shirts, a few sweaters and she piled them all in front of me. She held some of them up to me in front of a mirror, so I could see how it looked. I tried on a whole bunch of stuff. She must have thought she was doing something good, because she stayed with me the entire time, even waiting for me to come out of the dressing room.

"Oh, that looks good," she said, adjusting the waist of the pants and then standing back and examining me. "But you really need to get them a bit tighter."

"I like them loose," I said.

"Yeah, I know. Take my word for it. They look ridiculous. I'm sorry. I'm being so blunt, aren't I? My friends tell me that's my biggest character flaw. Anyway, pants can be loose if it's the style, but not loose like that. I think you should wear your size. You know what I mean?" She looked at me, hands on her hips.

I ended up buying a couple pairs of pants and three shirts. The girl was putting them in big Gap bags, but she stopped and looked at me like she had something important to say but didn't want to hurt my feelings.

"Just be blunt," I said.

"You should wear one of your new outfits out of the store."

"Outfits?" I said. "They're just clothes. I don't wear *outfits*."

"Okay, new clothes then. Why don't you wear them now? You look really good in them."

I went into the dressing room and put on the new clothes. When I got out, she put my old clothes in one of the bags. She walked over to me, reached for my leg and pulled a sticker off of my jeans.

"So why the new look all of the sudden?" she asked.

"I don't know," I said. "I think my girlfriend will like it."

"That's nice," she said. "You seem like a really nice guy."

I thanked her and walked out of there in new pants and a short sleeve, button-down shirt, which was bright blue. She watched me walk away, as if she were a proud mother sending her kid off to school. I guess I felt pretty good. I had one bag of new clothes and one with my baggy, Ben Davis, work pants. I don't know why I did what I did, but I dropped the old clothes into the garbage and walked out of the mall.

When I got home, Jessica stood up from the table where she was working and she put her hands over her mouth. "Oh, *m'ijo*. You look so good!" She just stood there looking at me, nodding her head in approval. "You're very handsome, did you know that?"

I told her about my plans to take Iliana to San Francisco, and she said absolutely not. She told me she wasn't going to have me stay in some cheap motel with some cheap girl (for some reason I would never understand, Jessica didn't like Iliana), but I was persistent. I kept begging her.

I told her that I wanted to see the paintings with Iliana, because together we could talk about them, and that way, when I got home, we would be able to analyze the techniques together. That would help me to remember and to apply them to my own work.

I told her that I needed some sort of push or I was going to keep painting the same stuff over and over again. I was good at lowriders and stereotypes, but whenever I tried to do something non-Chicano, I had trouble getting it right. I told her I wanted to quit glorifying the gang life, that I wanted to be more than just a Chicano artist.

"I'm ready to start a new life," I said holding out my arms, indicating my new clothes.

"I think painting is a good hobby for you," she said.

"So can I go?"

"Okay, but if that girl is going with you, you have to stay somewhere under adult supervision."

"We don't know anyone in San Francisco."

"Your cousin Johnny lives in Berkeley."

"He lives with my *tía*."

"Not anymore. He has an apartment."

Those were her terms if we wanted to stay the night, so I called him.

"Hey, Johnny," I said. "This is your cousin Victor."

"Well if it isn't the cholo," he said. "I can't bail you out of jail, so call someone else."

Friday morning I picked up Iliana at her house. It was so early that it was still dark outside. But I stood outside of the car, leaning against it, wearing a new pair of pants and a bright orange shirt. She walked out of the house unhappy, as if she were going to the hospital. When she finally reached the car, she didn't notice my clothes. She just got in the car and slammed the door shut. I got in the driver's seat and leaned over to kiss her. She offered me her cheek, reluctantly, like a little girl who didn't want to be kissed by her uncle. Her arms were even crossed, like she was angry.

"Something wrong?"

"Just drive," she said.

I didn't move, I just sat there looking at her.

Her eyes were puffy, and her lips were more pouty than usual.

"What's your problem?" I asked.

"You better just get the damn car on the road," she said, "Or I'm going back inside."

"What the hell?"

"I'm serious, Victor."

"Whatever," I said, shaking my head, as if I couldn't believe she would act that way. I started the car and pulled onto the street.

She slept for the first hour.

I was angry, because the whole point of her coming with me was that we could be together, do stuff together, talk together, and here she was just sleeping like I wasn't even there.

Along the highway there was nothing to look at but a bunch of farms and cows, all the small towns where no one would want to live.

I put on the stereo to let some Death keep me company if she wasn't going to. It was some underground group I liked.

Let the dead bury their dead!
Let the dead bury their dead!
Tell all the dead . . .

I moved my head back and forth like a lead singer. I pictured me on lyrics and the rest of the band in the backseat, a ghoulish looking bunch, on drums and guitars.

She had been asleep, totally out of it, facing me, her hands snuggled into her thighs. But when the music blasted, her eyes popped open. "Turn that shit off!" she yelled.

Those were her exact words, and stupid me acted all scared. I reached for the button and turned it off.

The ghouls in my backseat disintegrated into light particles.

She wasn't usually like this, but we had never spent the night together. Seeing what she was like in the mornings was seeing a part of her that I had never seen before. Now I could see it. If we were going to be with each other for the rest of our lives, then I was going to have to accept her, even this part of her.

Maybe that was what love was all about. Maybe love is not thinking that the other one is perfect, but it's loving them as they were.

Like Jessica.

I didn't know what Jessica felt for the old man. I didn't know if she loved him, but there was something about their relationship that worked. There was peace at home, probably more so than there ever had been when she was with my father.

Living with the both of them wasn't bad at all. In fact, I was kind of happy about it. Maybe there was peace because she accepted that he was an old man who was ready to quit working and enjoy the rest of his life. He drank a lot of beer, watched a lot of TV and he gambled, but that was all right with her. She didn't expect him to be anyone else.

He also accepted who she was. She needed control. She needed things to be her way, and he accepted her rules. He couldn't drink more than a six pack a day. If he did, she got angry at him. She let him gamble, but he had a monthly gambling fund. She put limits on parts of his life, and he accepted them.

In spite of who she was in the morning, Iliana and I were a perfect couple. I decided that when she woke up, I wouldn't be mad at her.

Then she woke up.

Her eyes blinked open, and they looked bright and wide. She said, "Good morning."

"Yeah. Great," I said, still mad in spite of my efforts not to be.

Then she sat up, stretching her upper body as if to get a better look outside. "Where are we?"

"Just outside Los Banos."

"How long was I asleep?" she asked.

"About six hours," I said.

"I didn't sleep for six hours," she said. She reached for the stereo and turned it on. Death blasted into the car.

I hate you.

I want you

I hate you

You're dead.

"I can't believe you listen to this crap," she said.

"You just don't understand it," I said

"What's to understand? It's a bunch of screaming. They sound like monsters and ghouls."

"Exactly, the screaming dead. There's a reason the voices are like that. You *feel* them with your body."

"Well, I'm not into talking to the dead."

"Sometimes they talk first," I said.

"Silence is golden," she said.

The road was a four-lane highway, two lanes each way, but there weren't many cars.

"Let's do something," she said, sitting up in her seat. "Some sort of travel game."

"We can time travel," I said.

"Know of any wormholes?"

"They're everywhere?" I said.

"Show me. Show me."

"Here we have a . . . " I looked across a stretch of land, fields of yellow grass at the end of which was a white house shaded by eucalyptus trees, and in front of it was an old pickup truck.

"There's one," I said, pointing.

"Where?"

"That house. The truck. That image."

"Reminds me of the house I walked by on the way to school when we lived in Visalia. We lived out in the country."

"Exactly," I said. "It's a wormhole. You just time traveled to when you lived in Visalia."

"That's not time travel. That's remembering."

"But it *is* time travel. It's just not how scientists thought it would be. Every image is a wormhole. We see something that grabs our attention and we remember things. We go back in time."

We passed a farm, and there was a white horse under a tree eating grass, a bird on his back, just hanging out.

"There's another one!" I said. "That horse can take us to a memory, or it can makes us think of the old west, where there's a horse under a tree with a bird on its back, just like that one. It's a passage to another universe. Or we might say to ourselves, 'One day I'd like to get a horse,' and we picture ourselves as some day having one, and we travel into our own futures."

"Well, not really the same thing as a wormhole," she said matter of factly.

"Wait, listen. Have you ever heard of the Law of Conservation of Energy?"

"Well, of course."

"My aunt Malinche told me about it," I said. "Energy never disappears: it just converts into other energy. If I look at a horse eating grass and you feel something, that feeling is energy, right? I can feel this sense of beauty

flow through me, my knees get weak, like when I saw
you for the first time."

She rolled her eyes.

"Well that energy is not created when I feel it. It has
just been converted from other energy, from another
time-space. When I experience that feeling flowing
through me, it makes me think of when I was a kid. For
little Victor in the past, those feelings I'm suddenly getting by just looking at something causes me to think
about the future. Both Victors are sending and receiving
energy through wormholes."

"Well, it's an interesting theory," she said.

We were overtaking a car on the other lane, because
it was going very slow. It was an old Toyota station wagon
sagging from its own weight. The driver was a man wearing glasses, and he had long hair like an ex-hippie. He
had a receding hairline, bald at the top of his head. He
was driving calmly, like he was in no hurry at all, windows rolled down, his hair blowing. On his stereo, he was
playing a song from the past, singing along with it,

Hello, lamppost!

What you knowing?

"That car is stuffed!" Iliana said.

That was when I noticed that the station wagon was
full of junk, clothes, furniture. There was even a trunk
tied to the roof where there were racks, as if he were taking all his stuff somewhere.

"Reminds me when of when we were moving to
Visalia," she said. "We drove there in a car like that. I was
seven years old."

"You just went back there. You just put the energy you
feel now into a wormhole, and I'll bet the little girl in that
car feels what you feel. She's probably sending the ener-

gy right back through, and that's why you feel something now, seeing the car."

"That's funny," she said. "I remember when we were in that car full of our stuff, or when I saw it parked on the street I wondered what our new lives were going to be like. We had lived in Los Angeles for the last four years, and I had to leave all my friends. I was thinking . . . "

"Of the future. Maybe that's why when girls get married, they often marry someone who looks like their father. When they see their future husbands, they feel something strong. That feeling goes back in time when they were little girls with their fathers, when they felt security or love or whatever it is one looks for in marriage."

"*Ay, Papi!* I think you're kind of turning me on."

She kissed me on the face as I tried to drive.

We entered the city of Los Banos. The traffic in town was slow that morning, cars and diesel trucks moving along in both directions. We looked at things and people like we were time traveling.

"Every image is a wormhole," I said.

"I concur," she said.

"I am a concurring current. Of hot, boiling love."

She punched me on the arm. "You are the corniest man I know."

"Even cornier than the *elote* salesman?"

"You mean the *elote* monger?" she asked. "As when Hamlet says to Polonius: '*Excellent well! You are the* elote *monger!*'"

"You know my favorite line in all of Shakespeare?" she asked. "It's when Ophelia goes crazy and sings, *Hey, noni noni! Hey, noni noni!*"

"Shakespeare sucks!" I said.

"How dare you say that!"

On the side of the highway I saw an old man riding a bicycle. He was pedaling ahead of us, going in our direction.

On the back of the bike there was a watermelon strapped with a bungee cord to a metal rack. It looked kind of funny, the wobbly old bicycle, the skinny old man. He was wearing shorts and no shoes, and he seemed to barely have enough strength to keep the bike going.

Maybe the watermelon was balancing the weight of the bike, and without it on the back, he would have toppled over.

"I'd like to draw him," I said.

"Then do it," she said.

The old man turned down a side street lined by tiny houses with big yards, poor people's rural homes. Snarling dogs behind chain-link fences tried to get at him. They were mean looking too, because a lot of barrio people liked to have mean old bulldogs and Rottweilers. The old man kept pedaling along like nothing bothered him. He looked peaceful, as if the best thing he could do in life is ride home on his bike with a watermelon strapped to the back.

I followed slowly behind him. The watermelon was held to the rack with a red bungee cord. We slowly passed him, but he didn't seem to notice us. His skin was dark brown and leathery, like he had been working in the sun all his life. His face was all wrinkled too, framed like a portrait in my car window. You couldn't tell if he was Black, Mexican or Asian. He could have been Filipino or Vietnamese.

On a distant corner, there was a Mexican grocery store that wasn't open yet. There were no cars parked out front. I accelerated, leaving the man far behind. I parked the car in front of the store. I pulled out my pad and got a quick sketch of him coming up the road. It was from a perspective where you see him coming right at you, his head an almost perfect circle, and you see the oval of the watermelon on the back poking out on both sides. I wanted to get a side view as well, so I sketched quickly and then started another one. It was hard to get him, of course, because he was in constant motion, but I drew a few quick sketches, capturing the movement of the spheres of watermelon and tires and the spherical head of the old man.

Geometry in motion.

I figured I could draw it with more detail later on. I loved that you couldn't tell what race he was, because there was something beautiful about that, as if the image carried its own lesson. It said, *When you get that age and have little life left over, it doesn't matter what race you are. All that matters is getting home and eating your watermelon.*

We were late to the museum, and Mr. García was angry. I told him that we had taken a wrong turn, and there had been an accident. We finally found the right way, but the traffic was bad. There was nothing we could have done about it.

"Well, fine," he said. "At least you're here. Now, come on, I want to show you an artist. Follow me."

"Where are the rest of the students?" I asked.

"They're being given a tour by a docent," he said.

We followed him. Iliana looked at me, and then she looked again. She noticed something about me, so she stood away from me and looked at all of me in my new clothes. "Wow! You look nice."

I shrugged, as if to say, *No big deal.*

"Does this mean you're not going to be a cholo anymore?" she asked.

"I was never a cholo," I said.

"I really like it, Victor!" She grabbed my arm and we walked together, following García. When we reached the room he wanted me to see, he stayed at the door and let us go in by ourselves.

I walked in hoping to see great art, like a Rembrandt, but what I saw instead was an exhibit of some artist named Wayne Thiebaud. I stood frozen in the middle of the room, looking around at cartoon pies and cakes on pastry shelves and ice cream cones with cherries on top. They were cartoons. This Wayne was pretty lame.

Why waste the museum space on art like this? I laughed and turned to Iliana. "This is supposed to be art?" I shook my head and mouthed the word *pathetic.*

"I have a great idea," she said. "Let's walk around the room in opposite directions. We'll walk right by the paintings without stopping, unless one of them strikes us. Then we can stop."

"Strikes us in what way? If it's good? If it's ridiculous?"

"It doesn't matter. For whatever reason. Just don't stop in front of a painting unless you want to stop. And we'll meet at the same place we started."

"Yeah! We can pretend like were on a train, and the paintings are what we see out the window. If we want to stop and see one in more detail, we'll have to get off the train."

"Sure, that'll work," she said.

I was a train. I even thought *choo choo* as I slowly chugged along, passing by painting after painting. I was amazed at the simplicity of the work. *Even I could do this,* I thought.

I passed by *Rivers and Farms,* which was an aerial view of an agricultural valley, but it was a cartoon so I didn't stop. I walked by *Three Cows,* and the three of them, almost identical, were walking down the incline of a hill, like cows from a comic strip. Wayne was lame. So I didn't stop.

Suddenly, the train stopped on its own.

I found myself in front of a painting called *Three Machines,* three bubblegum machines standing side by side. I wanted to dismiss it as a stupid painting. I wanted the train to hurry up and get going, to get back on track, but I stood before *Three Machines* and stared at them. Later on, I would Google it: *Three Machines. Wayne Thiebaud.*

It made me feel sad. It was a happy painting, but it made me sad.

How could three bubblegum machines affect me like that? I had to figure it out.

The machines were shaped like space helmets from an old-fashioned science fiction movie and filled with brightly colored gumballs, red, orange, blue, black, yellow.

I looked around for Iliana because I wanted her to see it too, but she was standing in front of a painting and staring at it. I went over to her and grabbed her hand. "You have to see this."

But she didn't budge.

She was looking at a painting called *Ballroom Couple,* a man and a woman with their backs to us. They stood on a shiny, dance floor, her in a strapless dress and he in a suit.

"That's pretty good," I said.

"It's so violent," she said.

I stayed silent, because I didn't see what she was seeing.

"Look at the woman," she said. "See how she looks down to the floor? It's like she's been beaten down so many times and she's submissive. And look at the man. Look how old he is compared to the girl. You can't see her face, but she's a brown woman. You know what? She reminds me of your watermelon man."

"My watermelon man?"

"Yeah, she's like your watermelon man. Now that I think about it, I'm a watermelon girl. Lot of people think I'm Asian. Some think I'm Indian or Arab. Look at her. You can't tell if she's Latina or Native American or Asian. She could even be black. Look how she carries herself. It's almost as if she's tied by the wrists."

Maybe this should have been obvious to me before, and maybe I only knew this instinctively, but maybe a painting was a story about to happen, or a story that had been going on long before you got there.

"The question is," said Iliana, staring at *Ballroom Couple.* "Is it sexist or a commentary on sexism?"

I walked back to the *Three Machines.*

Now I just wanted to see.

Each of the machines had holes from where the gum would come out. The holes were shaped like mouths, all of them making an expression like an *OH!* Those mouths made the machines come alive. They were screaming at me.

I imagined the yells, *Ahhhhhhhhhh!* And the gumballs started shooting out at me—one-at-a-time—pth!-pth!-pth!—splattering all over my face and chest like paintballs. I tried to protect myself with my arms, but the machines kept rapid-fire shooting at me.

There was so much traffic that it took us a few hours to find my cousin's apartment in Berkeley. Jessica kept calling and asking where we were. To prove we were still on the road, I held the phone out the window so she could hear the traffic: horns, sirens, the air brakes of diesel tucks. By about 9 p.m., Iliana and I finally found ourselves at his door.

"Get ready," I said to her. "He's kind of weird."

I rang the doorbell.

He answered, a big, white man filling the frame of the door. He had gained a lot more weight.

"Jessica has wisely entrusted me with your questionable chastity," he said as he let us in. "So don't even think of sleeping on the same side of the room."

The rest of our trip to San Francisco sucked.

Johnny took off the weekend to spend with us, and he treated us like we were babies. Iliana wanted to go to the Mexican museum to see the Frida Kahlo exhibit that was only there for another week.

"Frida Kahlo? I think not," Johnny said. "She's the most overrated artist who should have never been included in any museum. Only political correctness has got her labeled as great painter. She's a self-absorbed idiot."

"What?" Iliana yelled.

Those were fighting words.

"She only paints herself because she has no other vision. She's the selfie artist."

"You don't know what the hell you're talking about."

"The only reason she's famous for her pathetic art is because feminist Latinas needed someone to admire. You know who *was* a great artist? Her husband. She should have stayed home and cooked for him."

"How could you say that!" she asked.

I think he was enjoying making her angry. In his own weird way, he was flirting with her, but this was the best that he could do, deliberately acting in a way that he knew would inspire intense emotion within her. He wanted to connect to her, and who could blame him for wanting to feel emotional intensity with her? I wanted the same thing.

But she was pissed.

Johnny had a one-room apartment, so it didn't have a bedroom, just a main room, a kitchen and a bathroom. We all had to sleep in the main room, Johnny on his futon and Iliana and I on the floor.

He made us sleep on opposite sides of him. We couldn't even see each other; he was so big, like this massive object between us, a mountain range or a fallen giant. The air in the apartment was heavy, and it smelled pungent, like rotting green vegetables.

That night, he started to snore. We scooted across the floor so we could be near each other. We were lying on our sides, facing each other. She whispered, "This guy's a nut."

He stopped snoring, so we froze and waited.

He was sleeping on his back.

The snoring started again.

"I'm sorry," I said. "He's my *primo*."

"Let's ditch him tomorrow," she said.

"Jessica said I have to call as soon as we leave. We wouldn't be able to stay in the city."

"I don't care. I just want to get away. Besides, the drive home will be fun." She kissed me on the nose, and she left her lips there, so when she spoke I felt them moving. "We can stop in Los Banos again. Maybe we'll see the watermelon man."

We kissed, but Johnny stopped snoring. We were frozen in each other's arms. He let out a massive sigh and rolled over on his side, facing us, but still asleep.

We silently slithered back to our opposite sides of the floor.

⁂ ⁂ ⁂

The next morning, when we woke up, Johnny was already dressed and cleaned up. He looked like a little boy going to church. He wore a pair of black sweatpants and a clean T-shirt.

"Today, we're going to see some architecture sites throughout the city. Maybe you wanted more of your *ethnic* art, but I'm seizing the opportunity to educate you little snuggle bunnies. Get dressed and let's go."

He was by the door, eager to go, a camera hanging around his neck.

"We're going to drive back early," I said.

"Why?"

"Iliana's not feeling very well."

He looked at her. She held her stomach, as if she were nauseated.

"I'm calling Jessica," he said.

"Oh, yeah, thanks for reminding me," I said. I called her on my phone. I told her everything was all right, but we were driving back early. I handed the phone to Johnny.

"Hello, Jessica," he said. "Yes . . . I suppose they have behaved as best they could. But if the girl is sick, I'm not sure it's a good idea for her to be traveling in a car. Maybe they should stay here until she feels better."

"No!" said Iliana. "I need to get home. I need my medication."

Johnny handed back the phone. I told Jessica I would call her when we reached Fresno. I got off the phone and asked Iliana if she was ready to go.

"Yeah, I am," she said and walked out the door, down the sidewalk and was already at the street.

"She's really not feeling well," I said.

"Well, you're missing out," he said, standing by the door like he wanted to come with us. "I was going to show you some cathedrals and some quite interesting architectural sites."

"Next time," I said.

I hid behind the door so Iliana couldn't see me, "I got something for you," I said. I pulled a little baggie out of my sock and handed it to Johnny. "For later," I said.

"Thanks!" he said. "But you know this is *Berkeley*."

I gave him a hug and three hearty pats on the back. "We'll see you, *primo*," I said.

"I suppose it wouldn't be too intolerable if you come back again," he said.

He watched me walk all the way to the street where I had parked my car. Then, when we got inside, I waved. He nodded his head and closed the door.

"Thank God!" she said as we drove into traffic. "To quote Dr. King: *Free at last!* That man is intolerable."

"Ah, he's just a little set in his ways," I said.

"Victor, what were you doing just now?"

"What do you mean?"

"You seemed to be hiding behind the door."

"Oh, no, I was tying my shoes."

"You're not still doing marijuana, are you?"

"You don't *do* marijuana," I said. "It's not like heroin. You smoke it."

"You don't still *smoke* pot, do you?"

"Of course not."

"I don't want that in our lives," she said.

"Me neither."

She put her head on my shoulder. I loved how fresh her hair smelled. I kissed her on the head.

"But just to clarify," I said. "What is it about pot that you're against? I mean, the research shows that it's not bad. No worse than alcohol."

"I wouldn't want you drinking either. Look, we have endless debates about this in forensics. The bottom-line, Victor, is that pot may not be harmful to adults, but to teenagers, people our age, it actually slows down the growth of new neurons in the brain, and it can make you dumb. You start forgetting things. It kills young brain cells. When you're 30, 49 years old, do what you want, but at your age, it slows the growth of your brain."

⁕⁂⁂ ⁕⁂⁂ ⁕⁂⁂

Mr. García showed me around his house, the bath-room, the kitchen, and he told me I could use whatever I wanted. There were only two rooms that I wasn't allowed to go into: his bedroom and a room at the end of the hall that he said was always locked anyway.

"What's in there?" I said, looking at the door gleaming at the end of the hall.

"You don't want to see it, believe me."

"Is it something bad?" I asked, picturing the dead bod-ies of past students he had invited over, maybe some of them still alive and chained to the wall.

Earlier that week, he had asked me where I painted. I told him in my backyard, behind the clothesline. He offered me studio space in his home, but he asked me not to tell anyone from the school about it because it might look suspicious to a sick-minded world.

"Are you like a crazy axe murderer or something?" I said now, looking at the locked door at the end of the hall.

"They're my paintings, Victor. I closed the door on them a long time ago."

"Can I see some?"

"No, you can't."

I went there almost every day, painting in his glass-encased studio. He had everything I needed: easels, oil paints, canvases. He told me that he didn't use the stuff anymore, so why let it go to waste.

His house was cool.

Rich, too, like he must have bought it years earlier when real estate was still affordable, because now the house must have been worth a lot more than a school teacher could afford. He was probably the only high school teacher in the neighborhood of lawyers and business executives. It was in the Woodward Park area, and all the streets were lined with giant pine trees like at a resort in the mountains.

He had paintings all over the walls, original oil paintings and watercolors. He said he had been collecting art for years, starting when he was in college and he exchanged work with his friends. He had so many paintings that art museums sometimes asked him to lend them some.

"Let me show you this one," he said, and we went back into his kitchen. The room was large and white with a lot of sun. He had a brass rack on the ceiling from where brass pans hung down. It looked like a kitchen from the movies.

"This place is nice, Mr. G," I said.

He shrugged and pointed to a painting on the wall.

It was a cartoon image of a slice of lemon meringue pie.

"Wayne!" I said.

"It's an original."

"It's probably worth a lot of money," I said.

"There's more," he said leading me into the living room. "Do you know whose work that is?" he asked, pointing at a painting of a landscape.

It was kind of weird, not quite a cartoon, but blurry, like a bunch of paint globs. When you stood far enough away, it was a landscape of a countryside and rolling hills and a dark, menacing sky. The closer you got to it, the more it just looked like undisciplined globs of paint, like blurry faces coming out of the canvas.

"That's interesting," I said, walking backwards and forwards to get the full effect.

"Do you know who that is?" he asked.

I tried to read the signature but it looked like a bunch of curves and lines.

"His name is Samaniego. He's originally from Chile, but he's been living in Paris for the last forty years. He's considered by many to be one of the greatest living painters. I got this one years ago. It was expensive back then, but now, now it's worth more than my house."

"Wow. I hope you have all this insured."

"Oh, Victor, insurance couldn't cover the loss I would feel if these paintings were gone. They *are* insured, of course, but that wouldn't make up for the loss."

"Of course not."

"Samaniego is connected to 'L'École des Beaux-Arts.' Have you ever heard of that?"

"No, never. I like the effect," I said, looking at the landscape, walking backwards and forwards.

"Why do you think he painted it that way?"

"I don't know."

"He's making a statement about reality, don't you think? Perhaps the things of this world only become real when there's someone to observe them and interpret that observation. When you look at it from close up, that's *real* reality. When you step back and you observe it, your brain gives form to all the blotches and *you* create a landscape. You, the observer, are giving form to reality, creating your own world."

"Sounds like solipsism," I said.

"Where did you hear that?"

"My girlfriend talks about that stuff all the time."

"Hmm. Well. Anyway, I'm sure you want to paint," he said. "Use whatever you need, okay?" He picked up an empty glass on the counter and put it into the sink. "And

Victor, if you run out of something, let me know. I'll pick it up for you."

"Thanks, Mr. García. Can I ask why you're being so nice to me?"

"I'm not being nice, Victor. I'm being supportive of your gift. Every artist could use someone who's willing to help."

Sometimes I painted while he sat in another room reading books or tending to his plants. Sometimes he would give me lessons on how to achieve a certain effect with certain brushes or a certain stroke. One time, he taught me how to use a knife, handy for creating straight lines like for the sides of buildings. He had all kinds of paintbrushes, some so thin you could hardly see the hairs, which he showed me could achieve transparent textures. He taught me how to paint light. And I loved to paint light, coming in from a door, shining on the face of an old man, sparkling on fingers that move across the black and white keys of a piano.

He must have trusted me, because he gave me a key to the house, or rather, told me where it was hidden: under a rock on the side of his house.

I kept trying to get *The Cholo Tree* right, but I thought I needed some practice doing trees. I drove around town with my sketchpad, looking for any tree that struck me.

I sketched a eucalyptus tree with tattered bark hanging from the trunk. I made it look a little spooky, corny even, like a ghost, and the tattered bark was tattered clothing. I sketched tall, palm trees with bad haircuts and cypress trees looking out over rooftops like giant children.

One day, I started adding puddles of water near the feet of the trees. That meant in one drawing I did two trees, the "real" one and the tree reflected in the water. Sometimes I put light sparkling at the tips of branches. Sometimes, in the reflections, just for fun, I would draw a person who looked like the tree. On the top, in the "real world," you saw a tree with its branches reaching up to the sky, but in the reflection, in the water, you'd see a person.

When I was a kid walking to school, I loved to stop at puddles and look into them. I saw the clouds down there in the belly of the earth. I saw upside-down trees. I saw my own face looking up (or was it down?) with awe. I wanted to dive into the puddle. I wanted to fall into the soft, leafy arms of the tree like children falling into the arms of God. I imagined the tree yelling, "Come on, jump! I'll catch you." I wanted to believe that the reflection in puddles was a world in itself, separate from ours but just as real.

Now, I kept drawing trees and puddles, and then I'd paint them in Mr. García's studio. I found something that helped me. Van Gogh wrote to his brother Theo that if an artist wanted to effectively paint a tree, he needed to see the humanity within it. I understood that, because when I saw two trees in a field leaning into each other, I saw two spirits wildly in love.

I went back to painting *The Cholo Tree*. I knew now that I was painting my father. He was the tree.

I put a puddle around his feet, and you could tell it was winter by the fog hovering over the puddle like swirls of smoke.

My father loved Sunday mornings.

He liked to make omelets for us. I would stand on a
chair watching him flip the eggs. He loved cooking,
maybe should have been a chef. After giving up his
dreams of studying math, he used to joke about someday
opening a restaurant. Maybe he would have been good at
it. He didn't have time to cook all that often, because he
was working 40 to 60 hours a week at the auto body shop.
When he did cook, he loved it. He used to like to joke that
Sunday was the day that he could step out of his "auto
body experience." He could spend hours making breakfast. One time he invented a breakfast, the "Eastside
Omelet," made with chorizo, weenies and American
cheese. It was the best thing I had ever tasted. I remembered that he was in a good mood when he cooked. He
acted like my imaginary friend Mario, the Italian chef.

When he made omelets, my job was to unwrap slices
of American cheese and hand them to him.

I watched him uncapping tiny jars of spices, sniffing
them: cumin, cinnamon, basil, mustard seed, saffron.
There were cloves, nutmeg and tamarind. He smelled
each one, trying to find the accent that he thought would
go best with the "Eastside Omelet." He choose cumin
After the omelets were cooked, we carried our full plates
to the table and sat down. My mom liked to sleep in on
Sundays, so she normally didn't eat with us.

It was just Dad and me. He sprinkled red drops of
Tabasco sauce over his omelet. I could smell it, and he
held up the bottle and offered to sprinkle some over my
food, but I whined *nooo.*

I held my arms protectively over my plate and he
chuckled. After we ate, I put the dishes in the sink. My
father took the straw broom from the corner of the room
and swept. I liked the sound of the broom.

He didn't know that two blocks away there would be police with helmets and rifles and that there would be hardcore bangers at the windows with shotguns. All he knew was that it was Sunday and we needed some groceries. This is what Jessica had told me, that he decided he would walk to the store. For some reason, he didn't take me with him. On his way back home, he ended up in the line of fire, although to this day I can't imagine how. Why would the police let him cross a crime scene?

My favorite part of Sunday was when I stood on the chair next to him as he made the omelet. He would take the fork and peel the fried American cheese that had oozed from the ends of the omelet onto the pan. He extended the fork toward me. "Check it out. This is the best part," he'd said, offering it to me. I'd pull off the fried cheese and eat it. It was delicious.

In *The Cholo Tree*, the tree had two branches—two arms reaching up to the sky. On the tree's massive chest there were carved initials of Chicanos who had hung around the tree throughout the years. In the fog that floated around the tree were the dead. All you could see was fog or mist. You couldn't *see* the dead. I knew they were there, somewhere in the blur of mist, somewhere on the other side of reality, but I wanted the viewer to *feel* their presence, not to see it. I hid faces in the fog, but so subtly that you couldn't say for sure they were there.

It took me two months to paint it, but when I was done, I liked it more than anything I had ever done.

I showed it to Mr. García.

He didn't say anything. His eyes traveled all over the painting. I suddenly felt stupid, like I was trying to be too spooky, like he saw right away that I was painting my father. It was silly.

"I'm just messing around," I said, as if I didn't take the painting seriously.

"This is the one, Victor," he whispered through his fingers.

"The *one?*" I said.

"This will get you into art school."

"You think so?"

He walked further away from the painting to get another perspective on it. He put his hands on his hips and looked at it. He nodded his head.

⁂ ⁂ ⁂

I wanted to paint Iliana, so I started to sketch her anyway I could.

I did her in a big armchair. I did her standing near a window in a yellow half top and jean skirt. Her short black hair looked spiky. There was so much sun that you could see the particles of light floating like lasers around her head. I did her studying, sitting at a table with her books open, baseball cap on, glasses on and a pencil in her mouth.

Mr. García didn't mind that she was always with me, and when we were alone in a room, he didn't try to act like a parent. Still, he was an adult, and I'm sure he wanted us to respect his home. Sometimes, when he passed by the studio he would look in, but he never bothered us.

I sketched her in a white summer dress, sitting on the couch, her feet up, reading a book.

One day Mr. García said he had some errands to do, and he left us alone. That was when I knew I was ready to paint her. The studio was glass encased and looked out onto his backyard, a perfectly cut square of lawn, flowerbeds with reds and blues and pinks, and there was an orange three and a lemon tree, the fruit heavy on the branches. His yard was surrounded by a tall, wooden fence.

Iliana stood in the middle of the studio. "How do you want me?" she asked.

"Green," I answered.

"As in näive?"

"As in, *I love you green.* Let's see . . . How do I *want* you?"

"Come on," she said, holding out her hand for mine. "Let's go into the garden. Bring the easel. Paint me there."

"Okay, Eve," I said. "Are we about to embark on original sin?"

We went into the backyard. The weather was perfect, not too hot, a slight breeze. The birds were singing in the trees, etc. In the distance, I could hear someone's lawnmower.

"How about there, in that lawn chair?" she asked.

"That's fine," I said.

She sat in the lawn chair and laid back, like she was at the beach or sitting by a pool, and then she faced me. She looked beautiful and healthy.

"I'm ready."

At some point Mr. García had returned, but he didn't come back there. When I was done for the day, we went back into the house and sat at the table and ate sandwiches.

"I should be hearing soon from Berkeley," she said.

"I already know the answer."

"Really? You think they'll take me?" she said.

"*Mensa* . . . I mean, Honey, it's a no-brainer. I got to get into to the Art Institute in Oakland. That's close enough to Berkeley."

"You should apply to a lot of places," she said and took a bite of her sandwich.

"Why?" I said. "I want to be near you."

"We're so young," she said.

"What does that mean?"

Mr. García walked into the kitchen. "Are you guys done with the painting?"

"It's turning out pretty good," I said.

"It's beautiful," she said.

He poured hot water into his cup, the steam rising up to his face.

⚜ ⚜ ⚜

Freddy wouldn't let me NOT enter the competition. It was an art contest. The city was doing a big celebration for the Fourth of July, and they wanted a local artist to create an image for the poster. The prize was $1,000.

We were at his house where he lived with his aunt. His parents had died when he was a boy.

It was a small place, and his aunt was sitting in an armchair watching TV.

We were at the kitchen table. It smelled like corn tortillas and salty pork boiling on the stove. He put the poster right in front of me.

Call for Artists, it said.

"I don't have a chance," I said.

"Who says? You got just as much chance as any artist. You're good, bro. One of the best I've seen."

"They don't want Chicano art."

"*¿Qué* they don't want Chicano art? Who you been talking to that you think you're not good enough? You should go to church with me sometime. *En serio.* God loves you, man. He didn't make you a loser."

"I'm still in high school. Can you imagine the artists who will compete for this?"

"I talked to your girlfriend, bro. *La* Hindu said she won't let you kiss her no more unless you enter this contest."

I painted a picnic at an inner-city park with a bunch of families, black families, white families, Latino families, Native American families, Asian families. Some families were watermelon people, like you couldn't tell what ethnicity they were, and they were all in the same inner city park: the kids running around playing tag, old people watching the action from lawn chairs, men playing soccer, teenagers kissing under the bleachers. In the middle of the painting, in the nighttime sky, there were fireworks blazing, but the only people watching the fireworks were a man and woman sitting on a red blanket in the park. Everyone else was playing, having fun, but those two were staring up at all the colors and lights.

I imagined that the couple on the lawn was Iliana and me. The fireworks represented our futures, all our hopes, all the things we wanted to become and to accomplish.

It was a family-based image, and it was the artist Carmen Lomas Garza who had given me the idea. She did paintings of Mexican families picnicking in backyards, or sitting on rooftops watching the stars, Mexican children playing on asphalt playgrounds, Chicano families sitting

around big dinner tables. Her art made me feel happy, so
I designed something like that for the Fourth of July contest. I called it *The American Dream.*

Then one day Iliana told me to come over, that she
had some news for me.

I picked her up at her house, but she wouldn't tell me
until we got "somewhere nice." We ended up getting a
teriyaki bowl and going to a park. We spread out a blanket and had a picnic.

"So tell me already," I said.

"I was accepted into Berkeley!"

"I knew you would!" I gave her a hug. "You're amazing," I said.

She got a full ride, too. I knew she was a genius, so I
wasn't surprised.

But she was surprised. She was buzzing with happi-
ness.

"I have to get into either the Art Institute in Oakland
or the art school in San Francisco."

She lay on the blanket, her head in my lap. Across the
park, some man was playing catch with his two dogs,
throwing the ball. The dogs ran for it, fought for it, but
only one of them could bring it back to the man, who pet-
ted the dog as a reward.

"You should do what's good for *you*," she said.

"What do you mean?"

"I don't know, Victor. What's best for you?"

"To be with you."

She sat up.

"I mean, we're young, you know?"

"What are you saying?"

"Nothing," she said. She put her head on my shoulder. "I'm not saying anything."

Then I got the word from the art school in San Francisco. The answer was a big fat *NOOOOOO*. They sent back my portfolio, which had pictures of my paintings, copies of my drawings and my artist statement.

That rejection depressed me.

I had to paint something good and update my Oakland portfolio. I'd send it to them and ask them to add it to what I had already submitted. If San Francisco rejected me—and they had all my best stuff including *The Cholo Tree*—then so would other places.

I spent all day and night at García's trying to paint a masterpiece, one image after another. But the greater I tried to be, the more average the painting turned out.

Then the really bad news came.

Oakland rejected me.

That was the biggest blow of all, and the rejections that poured in after that were like jabs to finish me off.

I didn't want to tell Iliana the bad news, because I didn't want her to think that she had been wrong about me. She thought I was a good artist. She thought I had a good mind. She believed in me, and now the truth came out.

I could have understood the rejections from the UC campuses, because my grades weren't good enough. My freshman and sophomore years, I got mostly Ds and Fs.

I showed Mr. García letter after letter. He plopped down on his couch and said, "I'm really surprised, Victor."

"I'm not," I said.

"Don't say that. You're a good artist who could be great."

"Bullshit."

"Don't take this to mean anything except these schools aren't for you, okay? They're not the right choice for you. That's all it means. You have to have faith."

"Faith? I had faith. What good did it do me?"

"Did you hear from Paris?"

"I'm not going to Paris."

"Did you even apply?"

"Why should I? I wouldn't go."

"I told you. It's the best art school in the world."

"Who told *you* that? White people?"

"What?" he sounded scandalized. "What does that have to do with anything?"

"I'm not going to study with those Euro-peons."

"Because of Iliana?"

"Because I have no desire to live around a bunch of stuck-up, baguette-eating Euro-Nazis. I'm a Chicano. I belong here in Califaztlán."

"Victor, do you know how ignorant you sound?"

"They can stick their baguettes up their you-know-whats."

"Iliana might be the greatest girl in the world, but she's only a girl. No, let me put it this way: She's only a girl in the same way that you're only a boy. She's a girl-friend. A high-school sweetheart. The chance that you two are going to be together for the rest of your lives is very, very slim. Even if you *are* destined to be with each other forever, going to a good school isn't going to change that. If anything, being at different schools will make you a stronger couple."

"*Amor de lejos, amor de pendejos,*" I said.

"That's not necessarily true," he said.

"What am I supposed to do? Let her go to Berkeley by herself?"

"Yes!"

"Leave her alone over there with all those smart guys?"

"Believe me, you'll have other girlfriends. Other loves that you'll think you can't live without. She's not as unique as you think she is."

"You going to talk shit about her?" I said, stepping up to him like I was about to hit him. He was sitting on the couch, and I was right in front of him, looking down on him.

"No, it's not about her. I'm sorry, okay?" He stood up. He faced me. "She's great, okay? I'm talking about you. You need to do what's right for you."

"Whatever," I said and I started to walk out of the house. "You might as well put all that shit away," I said. "I ain't painting no more."

"*Ain't?*" He said. "*No more?* What kind of language is that?"

"*Chale con* everything," I said.

"Victor, stop now. Quit acting like a tough guy that I know you're not, and listen to me. You wanted Oakland the most, didn't you? Call them. Ask them why you were rejected. Fight for your position, maybe they'll listen."

"I'm supposed to ask them why they hate my shit?"

"Call them, Victor. You have to find out why, so you can improve next time. Even if you don't make it this year, after a few classes at City College, you can apply again next year. It's no big deal."

"Not to you. You already have your nice house and cushy job."

"Oh, shut up, Victor. Call and ask them how they arrived at their decision. It's worth a try."

And I did, too, and I even got to talk to the head guy there, their main artist. He was some famous guy, who was supposed to be a genius.

I couldn't believe I had gotten him on the phone. It was by chance. He happened to be in his office when I called.

"Professor Green? I'm Victor Reyes. I applied to study at your school this year."

"Yes, I remember your portfolio. How can I help you?"

"I was, uh, just wondering why I got rejected. Were my paintings not good enough?"

"Well, I seem to recall that they were good paintings."

"I don't understand."

"Do you want the truth? I can be very frank with you, if that's what you really want."

"Yeah, of course."

"There was nothing extraordinary about your work. They were frankly stereotypical images of urban, Hispanic youth."

"I don't paint Hispanics. I paint Chicanos."

"Your craft is excellent. But a lot of your work is cultural stereotype. No one really cares about gang bangers."

"I'm not a gang banger!"

"That's not what I mean. I mean there are millions and millions of people who know how to draw. Some of them do it very well, but we don't look for people who

can 'draw or paint.' We look for gifted visions. We didn't
see that in your work, Mr. Reyes."

"So you saying I ain't good enough for your school?" I
said this in a challenging Chicano voice. "I ain't good
enough for your *gabacho* school? You think I should quit
painting?"

"Well, that's up to you."

I hung up on him before I threatened to go over there
and beat his ass.

I decided right then and there that I would give up
art. If I wasn't good at it, why waste my time?

Who needed another artist anyway? If you were to
gather all the artists in the world and all the people who
thought they were artists or who secretly wanted to be
artists—whether painters or poets or musicians—if you
gathered them all together and put them in a spaceship
and sent them to the moon, planet earth would have
about three people left.

Over 150 artists competed for that Fourth of July
poster-design contest sponsored by the county. They
chose a winner, four finalists and a list of ten honorable
mentions. Needless to say, *My American Dream* was not
on that list.

※ ※ ※

I knew I had to tell her the truth about me. When I got
the last rejection, I called her. I would tell her about all
of them at once.

She didn't answer her phone. I left a message, *Call me
back, baby.*

An hour later, she still hadn't called me back, so I left
another message, and then another. After several hours,

she still hadn't called me back. This wasn't normal. Usually she would at least text me, but nothing.

I drove over to her house. I parked my car on the street, which was lined with a bunch of beat-up cars. A gang of little Mexican kids was playing in the street, and some teenagers hung out on porches. I walked to the front door. I got this bad feeling that I shouldn't go any further, that I would find her inside with some geeky science nerd from Berkeley, a college boy. The house was small, and when you rang the doorbell a voice said, "Who is it? Who is it?"

Another one of her father's inventions.

No one answered. I went around the back and tried to peek into her bedroom. It was empty. Clothes everywhere.

I drove over to the house of the lady who sold me pot. She was about eighty years old and looked like a grandma. She was nice too, so I started calling her *la abuela*. She always had pots of food on the stove. Her fifty-year-old son lived with her. He was a gentle man who always got up from in front of the TV to shake my hand, and then he would go right back to his armchair while his mother and I did business. I usually bought an ounce, because a lot of friends relied on me to score them a little bag. La Abuela handed me a plastic bag full of buds and told me about how bad her legs were getting. I shoved the bag in my pants, kissed her on the cheek and walked out to my car. It would make the car smell like skunk for a week, so I opened the trunk and tossed it in there.

I wanted to do something. I wanted to call a friend, drink some beers, maybe walk around the flea market, but I had no one to call. I had spent all my time with her, so it was like I didn't have friends anymore. I thought of Equis and decided to drive to his house.

It was a small thing with a big porch and no lawn, just dirt, where a few old cars were parked, the tires flat. A big tree hung over the front porch. I got out of the car and walked to his front door. His mom answered.

She unlatched the screen door, came out and gave me a hug. She smelled like corn and lime.

"Is everything okay?" she asked. "How is my Harold?"

"I don't know, Mrs. Ramírez. I came by to see him."

She let me in and gave me cookies and *horchata*. She told me that he hadn't been home in about a year. She feared every time the phone rang or someone knocked at the door that he was going to be dead. "He's doing drugs, Victor," she said. "I don't even recognize him no more. He's so skinny, and he shaved his head! He started taking money from my purse. My own son, stealing from me!"

On the way out to my car I tried calling Iliana again. By this time I was pretty pissed off. "I don't know why you're doing this," I said, "but it's messed up."

I clicked the *end call* button.

I had nothing to do, nowhere to go. I pulled up in front of a liquor store and gave some crack junkie enough money to by me a bottle of booze. Then I gave him ten dollars so he could get some crack. I was almost tempted to go with him, maybe become a crack addict myself.

With the bottle between my legs, I drove around the city, taking swigs, wanting to feel drunk. I wanted to get so messed up that I didn't care about anything, but the truth was, I hated the taste of the booze. I wasn't having any fun at all. Drinking was only fun when there was someone to drink with. I only liked beer.

I threw the almost-full bottle in a garbage bin and went home.

I went into the backyard and started painting stupid stuff, not even planning it, just painting, following the brush and the colors more than an idea. I didn't want to be a painter anymore, so who cared if it was good? Good paintings mean nothing.

I just wanted to do something with all this energy messing me up inside. I didn't want to paint something "good" (obviously it wouldn't be good). I just painted. What else was there to do?

I must have fallen into a trance, because I painted for hours. I had to put some lights out there so I could see. I flooded the backyard with light. I painted and painted without thinking. I put on some music, real loud, head-banging Death. I guess it made me feel better to be in that zone. Or maybe I felt nothing. Or maybe everything I felt went into the image.

I ended up painting a gumball machine, just like the one Theibold did in his *Three Machines*. I painted one big gumball machine. Inside of it, I painted a bunch of multicolored gumballs, but I put something else inside of it, too.

I put a cholo.

He was screaming and banging on the glass, as if trying to get out of the giant glass bubble. The cholo looked tough, like a gang banger, and he was angry. He was pounding on the glass, looking like a bulldog. You knew if he got out of that gumball machine, he was going to kick some ass.

I painted all night long, in the trance most of the time. At one point, I got so tired that I had to sit down. Everything was spinning, and things began to get blurry. I was going to faint. I lay on the ground, right there in the dirt. I lay there scrunched up, holding on to my knees. I closed my eyes. Everything was spinning.

⁂ ⁂ ⁂

The next morning Iliana called me pretty early. "Oh, honey, I'm so sorry!"

I wanted to say, *Baby, I missed you*, but I knew I had to act a little mad at first. "Where the hell were you?" I asked.

"Don't talk to me like that."

"Where in the *heck* were you? I called you a million times."

"I know. I'm sorry," she said, but now she sounded matter-of-fact, not as sweet as she did at first. I wished I hadn't used the word *hell*. I tried to change the tone of my voice. "Baby, I was worried."

I think it worked.

"I know, honey. I'm sorry. It was my father. You know how weird he is. It was his whim."

"What happened that you couldn't even text me?"

"My battery was dead the whole time."

"You couldn't charge it?"

"Well, that's what I'm trying to tell you. Guess what we did? Guess where we went, the whole family, even my brother?"

"Wherever it was, they don't have phones?"

"We went to Berkeley! My mom and dad wanted to take me so we could look around at apartments and stuff, and guess what? They're thinking of moving there too. Maybe San Francisco, but you know how they can't stay in one place. They're thinking this is their chance to move to the city. Anyway, on the way there I tried to call you, but my phone died and I didn't bring my charger, I'm sorry. I always call you on my mobile, so I don't even know your number."

"You don't know my number?"

"When I call you, I call you by your name."

"That's messed up. You don't know your own boyfriend's phone number? Assuming I'm still your boyfriend."

"Stop it. Do you know *my* number?"

"Of course, it's 559 . . . "

"See?"

"Well, what are you doing today?" I said.

"Being with my baby," she said. "You want to go to your teacher's house?"

"Let's do something else. What time should I pick you up?"

"As soon as you can," she said. "I really miss you."

That made me feel pretty good. I guess it was hard to think of yourself as a loser if someone as great as her liked you so much.

I got off the phone, took a shower and got ready, singing all the time. I remembered the painting I had done the night before, with the cholo stuck inside the giant gumball machine. "What a stupid idea," I said to myself, and I started to feel depressed again, or maybe I just felt empty. I called it *Rage Against the Machine.* I knew it was a stupid title—because it already belonged to the rock group—but I didn't care.

When I pulled up to the curb, she ran out of the house. She was so happy I thought that I should wait to tell her the bad news about Oakland. I thought if she found out, she might love me a little less, a small amount at first, but eventually, she would figure she needed somebody as successful as her, not some barrio boy who couldn't even get into a decent college. I pictured her with someone many years older than her, a professor or a physicist.

She was wearing a jean skirt and a tank top. She didn't jump into the passenger's seat. She tried to open my door, and when she found that it was locked, she knocked.

"I missed you," she said, kissing my neck and my face. I guess it felt pretty good. She smelled good too, like shampoo. "I hate it when we're apart," she said.

"Is anyone home?" I asked

"They're all gone. Want to come in?"

"Yeah."

We went into her room, and she pushed some clothes off her bed and sat down. I sat next to her. I looked at the wormhole painting I had done on her wall, and now it looked so stupid, so amateurish. I remembered when I was painting it, how important it felt to be painting such an image, as if it mattered, as if my little painting contributed to physics itself, but now I could see what a quantum quack I had been. It was childish crap. No wonder all the schools rejected me. In my artist statement I had written about wormholes, and now I realized how stupid I must have sounded.

Sitting on her bed, she looked at me like she had something on her mind.

"I have something to tell you," she said.

"Here it comes," I said.

"I think my parents are serious about moving to the city. They think now's a good time, because that way I could live with them. I'm sorry, Victor. I know we were thinking about getting a place together, but this is what *they* decided. At least we'll be in the same place, you know? Oakland and Berkeley are like Fresno and Clovis. They're practically the same city. Things *there* will be just like they are here."

"Yeah, that sounds good," I said.

"And it's not like we *have* to live in the same city. You know what I mean?"

Something happened.

I stood up, as if someone was coming, ready for anything, but the room started to feel like it was getting smaller. I felt dizzy.

I could hardly stand up.

I couldn't breathe. I tried to take deep breaths.

"Are you okay, Victor?" she said, standing up. She wanted to reach for me, but she seemed to be afraid that if she touched me she would hurt me.

The room got smaller, not just the walls, but the smell, the heat, everything was pushing on me, pushing me into a smaller space.

I was trapped like a cholo in a gumball machine.

I saw my dead father walk out of the light.

M'ijo? he said. He reached for me, his arms as long and twisted as the branches of a tree.

Jessica was looking down on me.

"Are you awake?" she asked.

I looked around the hospital room to see if I could see my dad.

Outside the door, waiting in the hallway, was Jessica's husband, the old man Ernie Chávez.

"What happened?" I asked.

"That's what we want to know," she said. "Are you a drug dealer?"

"What are you talking about? Where's Iliana?"

"Do you sell drugs?"

"I don't know what happened."

"They found drugs in your car. You want to explain that little fact?"

The doctor came into my room with his clipboard. He looked like a doctor from an old movie, a tall, white man with the sides of his hair turning gray. He examined me, took my pulse. He smelled like new car leather and cologne.

"He's anemic. We'll give him some medication, some literature to read, but he should be fine if he takes care of himself."

He looked at me like a TV father. "You're lucky to be alive, son. You should have told somebody about this a lot sooner."

"You're testing him for drugs, right, Doctor?"

"We could look into that," he said. "But what we're dealing with here is low, red blood cell levels, dangerously low. He's probably known he's had a problem for a while." He looked at me. "Am I right?" he asked me.

I nodded my head.

"I want him tested," she said.

Here's what I think happened.

When I had passed out on Iliana's bed, she panicked and called an ambulance and they took me to the hospital. My mom and Ernie came over to get my car, and they searched it and found the ounce of pot. It was too much for anyone to believe it was my personal stash, and Ernie said I sold it or delivered it for someone else.

The doctor who tested me for drugs found traces of marihuana, and Jessica made sure Iliana's parents knew about it. Apparently, they spent some quality time on the phone talking about me. Iliana told them that she knew I used to smoke pot, but that I had promised that I wouldn't smoke it anymore.

When I talked to Iliana on the phone, she said, "Victor, you're a drug dealer! How could you?"

"Pot is legal in some places," I said.

"But it's not here, and you're selling it to kids, it messes up their brains. And besides, how can you say you're all for Chicano rights when you're doing the very thing that keeps us in poverty and violence."

"What do you mean?"

"You're a drug dealer! You make money selling illegal narcotics."

"Oh, come on!"

"And here's the worst thing: you kept it in your car, you probably had it in there when we were together. If you got pulled over and I was with you, I would be an accessory at best. It would be on my record that I was a drug dealer! How dare you gamble with my future like that!"

I had to admit to myself, she was right, she could have gotten into a lot of trouble. "I didn't think about that," I said. "I'm sorry."

"Exactly, you didn't think about *me.*"

"That's not what I meant."

"I think we need a break from seeing each other."

At that point, my dark energy kicked-in. I got angry.

She was using this as an excuse, because she wanted to break up and had hinted about it for several weeks.

"That's a bunch of crap," I said. "You're using this as an excuse to get rid me. Ever since you found out you'd be going to Berkeley, you knew you needed to get rid of me first."

"What are you talking about?"

"You don't need some Fresno Chicano boy to tie you down."

Like a lawyer seeking a fact, she asked, "Did you or did you not sell pot?"

"I wasn't really *selling* it selling it. Not for a profit."

"So who was making a profit? Whose profit was more important than our future?"

"You're a hypocrite!" I yelled, wanting to throw my phone against a wall.

"I got to go, Victor. I need some serious time to process all this."

She hung up on me.

Jessica fired me from the restaurant (she was afraid I would steal from the register for drugs). I could stay in the house until I turned eighteen, because of the law, but after that I was on my own. She didn't care what I did, whether or not I came home.

She reminded me of the time she had found a knife in my room. She had believed me once and look what she got in return.

She took my car away. She took my keys and locked the car in the garage. She also took my cell phone. I had no way of getting around and no way of calling Iliana. I wanted to walk over to her house, but something must have happened when I fell, because I couldn't walk all that well. I stayed home all day, all night. I missed a week of school.

By the time I was well enough to walk, I had nowhere to walk to.

I took the bus to school, but what was the point of my classes by now? I hardly showed up.

One day, I decided to cut school and take the bus to the other side of town and try to find Iliana. I staked out her school until I saw her. She was walking with some friends, the red-headed boy and the blonde girl with glasses. She was talking to them as they walked, holding her books in front of her.

She looked so pretty, so bright-eyed, so brown.

I followed her until one of her friends noticed me. "Your favorite, cholo guy is following us," I heard him say, and they all turned around.

"Hey, baby," I said to Iliana. I half expected that seeing me would dissolve all the bad energy between us, that she would run into my arms. I might have even held them out to her. "Oh, baby."

"You have to go, Victor."

"I'm sorry, baby. Please!"

"Don't try and see me, okay?"

"What?"

"I'm serious, Victor, please leave me alone."

"If you just let me explain. At least hear me out." I walked up to her, and I stopped right in front of her. She was so close I wanted so badly to touch her. "I can't paint. I can't think. Baby . . . "

"Don't call me baby."

"I promise you I only sold enough of it to have a little for myself, because it's so expensive, and I didn't think of what could happen to you, and I'm sorry. That was selfish."

"Victor, I know you're not a bad guy, even if I don't agree with the choices you make. Even though you lied to me, I know you're not a bad guy. But I need some time."

"You don't love me?" I asked, swallowing the saliva that was building up in my throat.

"I'll always love you. That's not the point."

"But . . . "

She ran away, back to the schoolyard, her friends following her.

"Wait!" I ran after her. "Iliana, don't do this!"

Suddenly I saw myself as a cliché, like I was some drunk, cholo guy at a party looking for his ex-girlfriend, a girl surrounded by her friends who wouldn't let him come too close. "Come on, baby," he'd say. "Don't be like that." He would have tattoos all over his muscular arms, booze on his breath, almost too drunk to stand up, and his face would be crunched up in despair. "You know I'm your *vato*, baby. Why you got to play me like that? I know you love me."

"Come on, baby," I said to her, as if I was too deeply into the role I was playing and it was too late to stop. Her red-headed friend said something to me like, "Go home, cholo!" I would never remember exactly what it was, just how it made me feel. It was like my inner Victor turned on a switch that instantly made me angry. I guess I had more rage in me than I knew was there. I grabbed the boy by the neck and threw him to the sidewalk like a life-sized stuffed animal. His nose was bleeding, and he was kicking his feet like an epileptic. Iliana came up and screamed to let him go and hit me on the back. The campus cops came up behind me with their sticks drawn, and one of them hit me in the back, knocking out my breath. I tried to stand up but another cop hit me in the back of the legs and I fell. Then they both hit me a few times on the torso and the ribs. It hurt like hell. I was handcuffed and they pushed me into a police car.

Jessica had to come and pick me up, and she was so mad at me that she yelled all the way to her SUV. "You almost killed that boy!"

She didn't unlock the passenger's door. She drove off and left me there. It took me three hours to walk home.

I knew that I needed to talk to Iliana to explain. I didn't know her phone number, it was in my mobile phone, so I sent her about a million emails, which the mailer daemon kept returning unread.

I didn't bother going to my high school graduation, but I got the degree in the mail. I opened the large envelope, looked at my name and tossed it all in the trash.

One day I was in my bed drawing crazy stuff, violent images and weird shapes, not even thinking about what I was doing. Jessica knocked on the door and then just walked right in.

"Your friend is here. Get rid of him."

"What friend?" I asked.

She slammed the door shut.

When I went out to see, he was standing on the font porch.

"Equis!"

He was *all* gangster now, but not one of those clear-eyed gang-leader types, one you knew you shouldn't mess with. He was a meth head. He was all skinny, all eye-popping out, but somehow, he looked better than me. He had a car, too. He gave me a Chicano handshake and a half hug. He didn't smell like his mother's kitchen.

PART FOUR
IN THE LAND OF STEREOTYPES

She said her name was Gracie, but she liked to be called *la* Baby Doll.

"*La* Baby Doll? That's not very original," I said.

"Well, that's me. Is that okay with you? Who do you think you are?"

I guessed her to be about thirteen years old. She wore jeans and sneakers and she swung her legs back and forth like a kid on a couch too big for her. She had a zip-up sweatshirt that said *la* Baby Doll in glitter. It was worn, and in some places the letters had lost their flakes. She was zipping and unzipping, nervously looking across the room to her sister Noni, who looked like a hardcore chola and who was now handing Equis a crumbled up ten-dollar bill.

"What do they call you?" *La* Baby Doll asked me.

I plopped down on the couch next to her. "The greatest human being that ever lived."

"You're so conceited. I can't believe it!"

She pulled the sleeve of her sweatshirt over her palm, and a few more pieces of glitter floated to the ground.

"You look like an aging Christmas tree, like when the tinsel falls to the ground."

She held up her hand, still covered with the dark green sleeves of her sweatshirt. "Quack! Quack!," she said. "Talk to the duck!" And she made her fingers move up and down like the beak of a duck. "Quack! Quack!"

"I'm going to call you Ducky," I said.

"No, really, what's your name?" she said.

"Damn," Equis said, un-wrinkling the bill Noni had handed him. "Where has this money been?" He looked Noni up and down. She was thick and masculine.

He handed Noni her stuff and she went to the couch and ordered her sister to move over, so *la* Baby doll moved close enough to me that our shoulders touched. Noni unwrapped her stuff.

She took out a glass pipe, put a little piece inside and lit it.

"Hey, Noni. Noni!" I said.

She ignored me, letting the smoke slowly come out of her mouth.

She must have been about 16 or 17. She had mean-looking eyes and tattoos on her wrists, tiny dog paws.

"Well?" asked *la* Baby Doll. "You going to tell me or what?"

"Tell you what?" I asked.

"You forgot? Your brain must be sleeping."

She snapped her fingers near my head. "Wake up!"

❄ ❄ ❄

I could barely tell the three dogs apart. They were anywhere from 17 to early twenties, and they looked alike to me.

All three were standing in the kitchen drinking beer, in a circle, all of them wearing tank top undershirts, all of them with thick necks and shaved heads, all of them with colors hanging out of the same back pockets, all of them with tattoos on their arms and necks. They did everything together: partied, ate, fought. Now they were in the kitchen talking and laughing.

There were a lot of people at the house that night, some on the back porch, some in what used to be a formal dining room. It was a beat-up three-bedroom, and some of the casement windows didn't open, so it got hot and stuffy inside, and there was no air-conditioning. There was worn, shag carpeting in every room, and the first time I walked in with my bag full of clothes, the place smelled musty, like mildew. I must have gotten used to the smell, because I couldn't smell it now.

The three dogs swiped each other's palms in a handshake and went to prowl around the party. When Equis had brought me there to stay, it was difficult to tell who lived there because there were always people partying at the house and crashing out on any free spot. But it was the three dogs, Equis and now me.

The three dogs always hooked up with girls who came to the house to party, and it looked like that was what they wanted to do now.

They were checking out Gracie, who was still sitting on the couch with her sister.

"Come on," I said to her. "I want to show you something."

She looked at me, as if she was surprised that I thought she would be dumb enough to go somewhere with me.

"Seriously. You can trust me. Come on."

I stood up.

She looked at her sister whose eyes were closed as she faced the ceiling, feeling the rush of the high.

"Hey, Noni, Noni," I said. "Come on. You and your sister. Noni, I want to show you guys something."

She mumbled something I couldn't understand then stood up and started walking to the front door. She was leaving. Gracie, happy to be leaving, stood up. She handed me the pillow. "See you later, alligator," she said, and they left.

"You wanted to get some of that, didn't you?" said one of the three dogs. They were all looking at me. I wasn't sure which one had asked me the question.

�֍ ✤ ✤

During the day, the three dogs slept or watched TV. The only junkies that came around were homeless guys who did drugs 24/7, and Equis had to deal with them. I smoked pot and took walks around the neighborhood or around the house. I didn't have a sketchpad or pencils or paint, so I started to do what Iliana had done with her non-camera. I imagined I had brushes and an easel. I saw things I wanted to paint and thought about how I would achieve the effect I wanted.

One morning I was wide awake and lying on the couch—all the guys were still asleep—I pictured Iliana walking in a white field in a white dress with a black camera. She was walking away from me, but then she turned around and looked at me, the yellow fields spread behind her, and she held the camera up to her eye and snapped me.

I put a pillow over my head and pushed hard, as if I wanted to suffocate myself. As my eyelids pressed against the eyeballs, an explosion of color went off in the darkness. It swirled and spread inside my head. I saw something forming, a dark landscape, like a field. I could make out two figures walking hand in hand, a man and little girl, like a father and daughter, just walking in a field.

That would make a good painting, I thought, and I looked around as if I might find a sketchpad, but there were just empty beer cans and ashtrays piled with cigarette butts. I thought, *where's my sketch pad,* and I wondered if I should get up and look for it. But then I remembered I didn't have one.

The summer was so hot the three dogs quit wearing T-shirts, but Equis kept his on. I think he didn't like the way he looked with a bare chest, because he was so skinny, anorexic looking. Whenever we saw him shirtless, we made fun of him. His acne had cleared up, other than the scars, but he had big cheeks that made him look like he was always smiling, like the kid on the cover of *Mad Magazine.* He always wore a big, loose T-shirt.

I walked around with no shirt as well. The three dogs had barbells on the back porch, and I started doing bench presses and other stuff. I used to workout with my father on his weight set in the garage. He'd play Oldies and spot me on the bench press, urging me to do more. "Don't be a little wimp," he'd say. "Push yourself."

Sometimes the three dogs worked out at the same time as I did, and we would spot each other, encourage each other like team members, *You can do it! That's the way!* We fist bumped each other.

It was always hot in the house, morning, day and night, so in the evenings, for relief, we hung out in the backyard drinking beer, barbecuing tri-tip. At night when it cooled down, everyone went inside and we partied.

Equis was like the funny guy of the house. He called it our Bachelor Pad and always said, "We living large!" They were small-time dealers and didn't make enough money to "live large." He always made us laugh. He was in his element. I started calling him Cantiflas, and the others started calling him that, too. I think he liked it. He had more confidence and sense of belonging than I had ever known him to have. Sometimes, he was even lucky enough to hook up with some girl.

The three dogs would often go out together and come back late, laughing and drunk. They would return with girls they had met at parties. When they left the house, it was just Equis and me, as well as anyone who came by to score or party or both. Mostly they wanted the hard stuff. But if someone wanted to mellow out and smoke some weed, I had enough to sell them, and I always had money in my pocket.

⚜ ⚜ ⚜

The next time Gracie came into the house with her sister, she looked almost happy to see me. A smile broke out on her face.

"It's Greensleeves!" I said.

"It's that crazy guy I met!"

It was slow that night, just a few people scattered around and the three dogs seemed pretty restless, like they all had massive amounts of energy that they needed to convert into motion. They were trying to get two girls to come into the bedroom with them for a private party. One of the girls wanted to go with them but her friend said it was too weird. "There's only two of us girls!" she said. "Why would we go with them if there's three?" "Get another girl," her friend said.

They looked around for someone else, but the only other girls there were Noni and Gracie. Noni looked like a chola version of Shrek, but Gracie was cute.

"Hey, come on," I said to her. "I want to show you something."

"Okay," she said.

I led her to one of the rooms, the one where Equis slept. There was a mattress with scattered blankets, and clothes were piled in a corner. The room smelled of dirty laundry and urine. There were pee stains in the carpet, from whoever had lived in that house before us.

"Come on, sit down."

I sat down on the floor against the wall. Gracie looked around. Over the window was a dark blanket, so you couldn't see in or out. She sat next to me. I had left the door open so she would feel safe, and Equis walked by. He looked in and said, "Be good now!"

I watched Gracie watch her sister, who was sitting on the couch smoking her stuff.

"Someday you should write about this," I said.

"What do you mean?"

"You should write a book about your life."

"Oh, my life! It's craaaaaazy."

She was trying to sound cool, street-style, but her voice was so tiny. She kept looking through the open door at her sister in the living room. Every now and then, Noni pulled out her little piece of plastic, unwrapped it and put another piece in the pipe. Then she rewrapped the paper and put it back into her pocket.

"What would you call it? The book about your life?"

"*Mi Vida Loca,*" she said, as if it were the most profound idea ever.

"Naw, that's too overdone. Everyone uses that title. You need something else."

"But my life is craaaaaazy."

I wanted to tell her to quit saying crazy like *craaaaazy*, because that seemed a bit overdone, like a stereotype. I didn't want her to be a cliché.

One of the girls in the living room fell on the coffee table and spilled a bunch of beers, and the others started laughing.

"See, I told you. My life's craaaaazy. I would call the book of my life . . . "

She concentrated by pulling the sleeve of her sweatshirt above her palm and putting it over her mouth. Then she bit the fringe.

"*The Crazy Streets*," she said.

"That's good," I said. "I like that."

"No, no! I got a better one: *The Street is Bumpity*."

"*The Street is Bumpity?*"

"*The Street is Hard.*"

"*The Street is Hard.*"

"Yeah, you see? The street is like my life."

"You like that title?" I asked.

"I do."

The three dogs stuck their heads into the door. "I got to talk to you, man," one of them said.

I stood up and told Gracie I'd be right back, but she got up too and walked out of the room and sat down on the arm of the couch, next to Noni. "Come on, sister, let's go now."

The dogs led me to the kitchen. Then they faced me.

"You want to do a run for us?" they asked.

"Yeah, sure," I told them.

They gave me the stuff and told me the place. I could keep 20 bucks for myself, they said.

"Cool," I said, and I started to leave. "Hey," one said.

I turned around.

"You got to leave now."

I looked in the living room at Gracie, and she looked up at me and made a gesture, circling her ear with her pointing finger, as if to say I was crazy in the head.

"I'm out of here," I said.

On my way out, I stopped at the couch. "You guys about to leave?"

Noni nodded her head.

"I'll walk you guys out," I said. "It's a bad neighborhood, and little girls shouldn't be alone out there."

"I'll mess them up," Noni mumbled.

She got up, and we walked out together.

The night was hot.

"Where you guys going now?"

Noni looked around, nodded her head. "Death, I guess."

"I hate when she says that," Gracie told me.

"Everyone goes there," she said.

Noni started walking, and her sister followed her.

She turned around. "See you later, alligator."

"Everyone says that. Can't you say goodbye in a way that only you, only Gracie would say it?"

"Okay, how about, see you soon, Sunny Moon!"

"Sunny Moon? Now that's something new. You invented that!"

"You're craaaaaaazy!"

When they reached the intersection, where there was a liquor store, they turned the corner and disappeared.

✤ ✤ ✤

One day I bought some pencils and a sketchpad. I thought that during the day while everyone else was asleep, I would draw. My "rent" was to sell stuff during the day, mostly to straight-up addicts, but I didn't get paid. I had a good hook up with La Abuela, and some people started to come by the house to score a bit of weed as well, and my roll started to get bigger and I started to buy larger amounts.

"Business must be good," La Abuela said. And she told me to sit down. She fed me chicken *mole* with rice and tortillas.

Sometimes it was frustrating dealing with daytime junkies, because they were mostly homeless guys who had been begging all day and night to get enough for a blast. They would hand me pockets full of pennies, dimes, nickels, quarters and an occasional crumpled up, smelly, old dollar bill. A lot of times they wanted to do their stuff in the house, but I wasn't supposed to let them.

Then I met Curtis.

He was a homeless, black man from Georgia, in his forties, and I wanted to draw him in my new sketchpad.

I listened to his stories as he smoked his stuff. He told me about boyhood memories, his marriage, his kids and how he ended up on the streets of Fresno. He was a decent guy. Every time I handed him his stuff, he said, "Thank you, Jesus," looking up into the sky. He was sincere about it too. He wasn't being ironic. He'd thank Jesus and then he'd do his stuff.

I sketched him.

He didn't want me to draw him doing a blast, he wanted me to draw only his face. It was like he cared about the pathetic picture I drew. I made him look regal, and he liked it a lot. It kind of freaked me out because it looked like my dad.

I drew stupid stuff, yellow flowers growing in weeds, the beaten body of an old washing machine on the porch, a cholo on the floor of the kitchen passed out and snoring. I drew a cat in the window. Drew some cholos hanging out in front of a liquor store. Drew bottles of beer on a windowsill. Drew a homeless man sitting against a wall hugging his knees. Drew Equis sleeping on his mattress, his automatic pistol resting under his splayed fingers. Drew a cholo ghost watching him sleep.

The wad in my pocket started to get so big that I had to find a hiding place. In the backyard there was a washing machine that hadn't been used in years. I reached my hand deep inside of its belly and hid my first wad of cash in there. After a while, I had to keep emptying my pocket. I put more and more cash in there and buried around the yard like drug lords in the movies. I was making more money than the dogs.

One night, some guy started freaking out, getting paranoid that they were putting something weird in his meth. He was a muscular, young giant, and it took all of us to pin him down and throw him out of the house. He got up and punched one of the dogs, so the three of them and Equis messed him up pretty bad. They kept kicking him in the head, in the ribs, and they invited me to join in, but I didn't.

Noni came over several times a week with bills crumpled up in her hands and buy her tiny piece and do it on the couch. Then she sat back and chilled, while *la* Baby Doll and I sat in the other room talking.

One night I asked if I could draw her. She said that she wasn't going to take off her clothes for me, if that was what I had meant.

I laughed. "Like I'd want to see a little skinny kid like you naked!"

She rolled her eyes.

"You're like my little cousin," I said.

"You think I'm skinny?"

She was sitting against the wall, her legs up and her chin resting on her knees. She had her sleeves pulled up past her palms. I pulled out my case. Now that I had money, I had been able to buy good stuff. I decided to do her in pastels. I started the drawing.

I remembered something Freddy had told me years earlier, when I had asked about Iliana. He said, "Every Chicanita is my sister," and at that moment I knew that I would kill someone before I let them hurt Gracie.

Things in the other room were starting to get crazy. Some guy who was scoring was hitting hard on some girls, and the three dogs were getting pissed at him.

"Not again," said Gracie. "Close the door."

I scooted my butt to the door and closed it. I went back and continued drawing her. I drew her watching the door, as if she were worried about what was happening on the other side.

"They closed the door!" someone said.

I continued sketching.

"So how come you're not at home studying or watching TV? This is a bad place for a thirteen-year-old girl."

"I'm not that old. Damn! I'm only twelve. And home ain't no better than here, or anywhere. All the *heres* in the world are better than *there*. My mom married a pervert. If you know what I'm saying."

"*All the Heres in the World.* Now there's a good title for your life story."

"Hey, Noni," I heard Equis say from the living room. "Your *hermanita's* getting some *chorizo.*"

"They're so stupid," Gracie said.

When I finished, I closed my pad.

She looked at me. "Well?"

"Well what?"

"Let me see," she said, scooting closer to me.

"All right," I said. I opened the pad and showed her the image.

"Wow," she said. "Dang! You're talented, big brother. I ain't never seen nobody that can draw like that." She put her head on my shoulder as she looked at the image.

"You can have it, if you like."

"You're definitely going to be in the book of my life. A whole chapter. I can see it now. *Chapter 13: The Crazy Guy I Met.*"

"Chapter 13? No, anything but that."

"You want to be chapter one?"

"Chapter 13 is what they call bankruptcy. You know, when you lose all your money." I thought about all the money I had hidden in the yard, how much it would suck to lose it.

"Well, then *that's* the title of my whole book, the book of my life. *Chapter 13.*"

I pulled her image out of my sketchpad.

"Don't tear it!" she said.

❉ ❉ ❉

One evening, one of the three dogs wasn't around, and the other two asked me if I wanted to go to a party with them.

Equis looked pissed off, because he knew someone had to stick around the house to sell the stuff. He went into the house mumbling something about bullshit. He slammed the screen door.

"I think he wants to go," I said.

"You want to go or not?" they asked me.

"Sure," I said.

Even though I was with them, I still could hardly tell them apart. I just started calling them homie.

As we got out of the car and walked toward the noise of the party, I realized I was one of the indistinguishable three.

I got an idea for a painting, all three dogs side by side, exactly the same, all of them trapped inside their own gumball machines, banging the glass to get out.

This party was crazy.

Or like *la* Baby Doll would have said, *Craaaaaazy!*

There were hundreds of cholos in the house, in the kitchen, the living room, coming in and out of the bathrooms and the bedrooms, and there were cholos in the backyard, on the patio, around the tree, drinking beer, taking long slow drags of cigarettes and blowing out clouds of smoke.

We three settled in the backyard, on the lawn by one of the kegs. Most of the guys were around my age, but some of them looked old, thirty, forty years old.

The old guys stood underneath a fruitless mulberry tree. The huge canopy of the tree made the yard a little darker. One of them, wearing a white, tank top under-shirt (not very original, I know) had his red bandana tied around his head old school style, pulled down so low over his eyes you wondered how he could see. He was an old stereotype, an elephant, a cliché. He must have been in his forties, and he had mean-looking eyes. As the other old guys were joking around, hitting on the girls, drink-ing beer after beer and passing around a bottle of tequila, this guy just watched everything.

More cholos came out of the house onto the patio and the lawn, and many poured in from the street through a wooden gate that was barely hanging on its hinges. Oth-ers came through a missing board in the fence, squeezing through the narrow slit like they had rubber bodies that inflated into people once they got to the other side. There were so many faces, so many shoulders, so many blurs of bodies.

Standing near us were two teenage girls and sur-rounded by about ten cholos, all of them hitting hard, the girls laughing as they held their wine coolers, raising the bottles to their mouths.

Couples were making out everywhere, against fences, against walls. The music was playing loud, the bass beat-ing loud, and all three of us *vatos* stood with beers watch-ing the action.

"Hey, Victor," a dog said. "Pull out a fatty."

"Do you share?" It was a girl's voice.

She was a short *güera* with blonde hair and green eyes.

"We do!" said a dog, and he closed in on her. She said her name was Yvette. She introduced her friend and the two dogs and the girls hooked up.

I stood there looking around. I noticed that when they came into the backyard, a lot of the cholos went up to the old men underneath the fruitless mulberry tree and shook their hands. The old men sat around the tree near a keg.

The backyard was so full that you could see blurs of bodies, but then something rippled, a wave of bodies. I heard yells, and there was a fight going on. All I could see was a pile of moving bodies, a dark patch moving over the darkness. A bunch of boys were jumping in and out of the center and the fight got bigger in mass.

Then we heard a gunshot and everybody started to run for cover, and people poured from the yard and into the street.

"Let's go," one dog said. "We'll party at our place."

We couldn't get out without passing through the fight.

"Cover your head," someone said.

And I entered into the mass of fighting boys, like I was entering into a dark and humid tent, and I saw a blur of faces, saw arms, saw fists, saw the back of necks and a shoulder smacked my chest, the blur of flesh rubbed against me, heat, sweat, any way you touched was sweat. I saw a face slide by, eyes red, looking at me like it wanted to kill me, and then it disappeared into everyone else. I felt an elbow on my side, so I hit someone, felt my fist hit a chest. It hit back so I hit again, felt a face, teeth, my knuckles stinging, felt an elbow at my ribs. I spun around, hit a face, my knuckles hurt, and we were all poured into the front lawn like bodies into a mass grave. I grabbed a guy flying by and threw him with his own momentum into a tree and I felt a sweaty arm choke my neck and spun around and I was an angel of death and I carried a sword and was slashing the heads and arms off of the cholos.

A girl ran by screaming, her lips red, and I pushed two guys running opposite into each other and one fell and the other wobbled and lunged at my chest with glitter in his hands and I pulled that arm and led the blade away from my belly.

"Let's go, man," said the dogs.

One of them grabbed me by the waist and ran with me like he was rescuing me from a fire. On the street people were piling into cars, trying to get out of there before the cops came. We could hear the sirens getting closer.

We got to the car with two girls, and a dog threw me the keys so I could drive. "Damn," the other dog said to me, "I didn't know you could throw down like that."

Throw down, I thought, then I remembered I was fighting. It didn't even occur to me I was fighting, as if I thought I was just walking through a storm.

I started the car and was about to take off when someone tapped on the passenger's window.

"Let him in," the dogs said.

It was an old guy with the red bandana on his head, pulled down over his eyes.

I reached over and unlocked the door.

The old guy got into the passenger's seat.

"I need a ride," he said.

"Sure, man. Wherever you want," the dogs said.

"Well, get the hell out of here," the old man said to me.

I pulled the car onto the street and got out of there. Cholos and Chicanitas were running all over the streets. One girl, running in high heels and a short skirt still had her bottle of wine cooler and she was laughing. She

looked in the windshield and smiled with red lips and
white teeth and blew me a kiss with her hand.

"Where do you want to go?" I asked.

"Clovis," he said. "The Flats."

"That's way over there," I said.

"What?" he asked, like he was about to smack me.

"Clovis is cool," said one of the dogs. "Go to Clovis."

So I did.

The old man pulled the bandana off his head. His hair
was pasted to his forehead with sweat. He spread the bandana on his lap. He pulled a small pistol from his waist
and put it on the bandana. Then he started folding it up.
He looked out the window.

"She better be there," he said.

"Who?" I asked.

He didn't answer.

"Are you going to see your girlfriend?" I asked.

"You a reporter for the newspaper?" He turned around
to the backseat. "Who is this fool?"

"He's our homie," the dog said. "He's all right. He just
don't know nothing yet."

We stopped at a light. We were the only ones waiting
there. The city was quiet.

I looked at the old guy. His eyes were wrinkled, he had
crow's eyes, but the orbs themselves were bright, because
the lights of the city were shining in them. I looked at the
gun on his lap, wrapped up in the red bandana.

"My name's Victor," I said.

He shook his head, as if I were an idiot.

The light turned green and I started to go.

"You better talk to this boy," the old guy said. "He's
lucky I don't cap his ass."

I laughed. It was a stupid thing to do, but it just came out, because it sounded so funny, "Cap his ass." It was so trite, so cliché.

"You think something's funny?" he said to me.

I tried to explain to him that the term *Cap his ass* had struck me, because as familiar as it had become in popular culture, it was surprising to actually hear it mumbled in an authentic situation.

"Damn, you talk like a professor," said one of the girls from the backseat, a short *güera* with blonde hair.

"I'm sorry. It just struck me that's all. No disrespect intended."

"What's your name?" he asked.

"Victor. Victor Reyes."

"Reyes?"

"Victor Reyes, Jr."

"Yeah, that's it! I thought you looked familiar." He seemed to relax a bit. "I knew your old man."

"What?"

"Yeah. He used to do auto body work on Belmont, *¿qué no?*"

"Yeah," and then it occurred to me that this *veterano* was my father's age.

"That was messed up what happened to him," he said. "I respect your father. He was all right."

"Thanks," I said.

"I was there when your dad met your mom," he said.

"What?"

"I knew that fool was going to marry her."

"You knew my mom?"

"Yeah, I knew Jessica. She used to kick it at all the parties."

"Parties? You mean, parties like tonight?"

"I was at that party the night they hooked up."

"I thought they met at the taco truck."

"How is your mother? She still like the life?"

"What do you mean?"

"She was crazy, man."

Craaaaaaaazy.

I couldn't help but picture Jessica like one of those Chicanitas at the party, dressed all revealing, maybe sharing a joint with my dad and then making out with him against a fence. I had always pictured her in youth as a traditional, Mexican girl. I had always pictured her in a pink dress and white socks. This was crazy.

Every Chicanita is my mother.

Both of the girls in the backseat were my mother.

The short *güera* was my mother.

I turned around to look at her, and it was Jessica!

She was making out with a Dog, his hands all over her. "Treat her with respect," I said, and they stopped kissing.

"What?!" asked the Dog, confused.

I pulled into a quiet, tree-lined neighborhood. You could hear our engine and the rubber tires slowly rolling on the asphalt.

The *veterano* directed me down a narrow road. "It's that house over there," he said, pointing at a little house with a porch light on, a dim yellow spot.

I stopped the car in front of the house. I turned off the engine, as if we would sit there for while. He put the wrapped-up gun into the waist of his pants.

"Thanks for the ride," he said. "Your father and I were tight," he said. "What he did for us . . . He took it for all of us. Know what I mean?"

"Not really."

It was an accident, I wanted to tell him. He was caught in the crossfire of a shootout. He had been innocently walking to the store to buy some American cheese, the individually wrapped kind.

"I got your back, you hear me?"

"My father was a gang banger?" I blurted out.

He got out of the car and slammed the door.

❋ ❋ ❋

What did he mean that my father took it for all of them?

He just ended up in the line of fire. That was what Jessica had told me.

If my father had been a gang banger and if the *veteranos* had my back, did that make me part of the family?

Was I born into this?

Were these my roots?

❋ ❋ ❋

When we got to the house there were a bunch of people partying, including the third dog. I learned two things about him that night: his name was Paco, and he hated me.

He had a scowl on his face and little eyes that shot from place to place like he thought everyone was a threat. His mouth had a scowl, and he had a wide forehead and looked like an ugly version of Quentin Tarantino. He looked at me as we walked into the house. "Where you guys been? Why did you take that punk with you?"

"You better chill," I said to him.

He was a pesky looking *vato*, like a weasel. "You ain't even one of us," he said.

A dog pat him on the shoulder and leaned into him. "I wouldn't mess with him," he said. "This *vato* is banger royalty."

"Come on," said another dog, standing with the two girls at the entrance to their bedroom. "Let's party!"

All four of them went into the bedroom and closed the door.

Paco looked at me, shook his head and walked out of the living room and went into the kitchen, where some other people were drinking beer.

Equis stood next to me. I looked at him and nodded, *What's up?*

He gave me the Chicano handshake. "So what's this about banger royalty?"

"I don't know. It's been a weird night."

"Hey, someone wants some weed. Can you hook him up?"

"Yeah, no problem."

My father showed up at the foot of my bed.

At first, I thought it was Equis, because I had slept on his mattress. I thought he was going to try and kick me out. I was about to tell him to get lost, but I saw that it was my father.

"Get up. I have something to show you."

I rose from the mattress and followed him. We went through the house. It was quiet and the only light was coming from the kitchen, shining on the walls and the hallway. The closer we got to the light, the more the scene became like a lit up stage. My father and I stood in the shadows and watched.

"Look at this," he said.

It was my father and me, when I was a kid. We're in the backyard of the little house he owned. Pepita was sitting on the back step, and she had her eyes closed, meowing as if she wanted me to pick her up.

We had on boxing gloves, and my father was on his knees, hitting me, punching me on the head and the ribs, and when I moved away he caught up to me running on his knees like a fast, little man. I was bawling and I just sat down on the ground and he punched me and knocked me over.

"Fight, you little wimp," he kept saying as he punched me. The little boy rose up and he was a man now, big and muscular. He grabbed the meowing cat and ripped her apart like a tough piece of meat.

I woke up. I sat up.

I was sweating.

I got up and went to the refrigerator for some cold water, but I heard voices, mumbles, curses, shouts. I could see now that the house was full of people. I didn't recognize any of them. I knew I was imagining all this, as if I was converting what I felt in that house into images. I must have been still dreaming. I couldn't think.

I saw several people, but they weren't talking to each other. They were all talking to themselves.

I heard one guy saying, "What's wrong with me?"

Another was sitting by himself on the counter, looking depressed. He said to himself, "Stupid, Stupid!"

I saw my father standing in front of me.

"Welcome to *Muertalandia*," he said, light coming from behind him.

"I should kill myself!" said the guy sitting on the counter, "That's what I should do."

"Who are these people?"

"The dead."

This big guy came up to me, like he was going to tackle me. He got in my face. "I'm gonna kill you!"

I stepped back, but my father laughed and said, "He can't touch you. He has no body."

The lights went out in the kitchen, and the light from the end of the hallway turned blue. We walked into it. We were walking on a narrow street lined by tenements and garbage bins like a trite scene from a graphic novel. You could see streetlamps and hear dogs barking. "This is what the dead see, when the dead see the city."

People were hanging out behind a trash bin. A crack pipe lit up the face of a man.

"They're harmless." He pointed to his own head. "The dead don't know they're dead."

"How's that possible?"

"That's what would have happened to you. If you had died that day. You wouldn't believe you were dead and you'd think your life just went on. You listen to me, *m'ijo*. Don't ever listen to the dead."

"But you're dead."

I woke up again.

I was soaking in sweat.

My brain was fried.

I tried to remember the rest of my days in that house but I only remember bits and pieces, because I was always stoned, and in recalling those days, I mix memories that really happened with things I only imagined, like my dead father. He didn't go away. He followed me.

One afternoon I was going to get something from the refrigerator, but when I got there Paco was sticking his whole body in there, like he might climb in and stay there. It was hot that day, and maybe it felt good, but he was standing there and I knew he had seen me, but he didn't care. That was when I saw it (or imagined it).

Paco was hanging out with dead cholos without him knowing they were there. There were three of them and they all surrounded him now as he stuck his head into the refrigerator.

They looked at me like they hated me. They said, "Get out of here." "I should kill you." "Who do you think you are?"

Paco kept looking in the refrigerator as the dead guys kept saying stuff to me. He didn't bother to get out of my way.

"Get out of the way," I said.

He didn't say anything, so I said it again, "Out of my way, bro."

I imagined my dead father standing next to me saying, "Get him, *m'ijo*. He's disrespecting us."

"Don't be a *pendejo*. Give me a beer," I said.

"Pendejo?" all his ghosts yelled. "You're going to die now."

He turned around. "What'd you say to me?" he asked, like he was challenging me, his lip twitching involuntarily.

My father whispered, "Close the door on his head."

I pushed him back into the refrigerator and slammed the door on his ribs. It made a lot of noise, and so did he. He yelled. Equis ran in and his mouth popped open. The *vato* came at me with all his weight. He was strong and wasn't wearing a shirt and all those sweaty muscles came at me and pushed me back across the kitchen and against a counter. He took a swing.

Everything slowed down.

I saw his fist coming at me in slow motion, and I grabbed it with both of my arms and twisted him around, using his own strength and redirecting the power so that he punched the cabinets, breaking them and scraping his own fist, which was bloody now. He screamed something, but everything was so slow that I saw his head was unprotected, so I grabbed it in my hands and smashed it into another cabinet. Then I pushed his face on the counter into a bunch of dishes, which shattered and fell to the floor.

I punched him over and over in the ribs and my father yelled, "Get him, son!"

The others were in the kitchen now, and they pulled me off.

"Damn, Victor," Equis said. "That's messed up."

I was breathing hard. Paco was on the floor, holding his ribs.

"I'm proud of you, *m'ijo*," father said, raising his fist for the bump.

I went to the refrigerator, grabbed a bottle of water and went out to the backyard. It was hot out there. I opened it, gulped it down and just stood there. My heart was beating fast.

Equis came out and stood next to me.

"Damn, Victor, you're crazy."

My father was sitting on the abandoned washing machine. "Kick his butt too, Victor."

"Naw, this is my boy," I said, and I gave Equis a hug.

"Forever," Equis said.

"Let them come," I said. "All they can do is kill me, *¿qué no?* I'm getting pretty good in the *ars moriendi*, know what I'm saying?"

"No. Honestly, no."

"It means . . . " and I couldn't remember, just that it was from some book I had read when I used to read books. It had something to do with the dead.

"The dead are everywhere," I said. "They follow us."

"What are you talking about, man? Earth to the cholo!"

When Gracie came over to the house with Noni, I saw the ghost following her. She was in her twenties, but she had bags around her eyes like she was older. She had flaming, red hair and wore a green dress. She looked like she could have been gorgeous at one time but had been doing drugs for so long she didn't care anymore. She was whispering.

That was when I noticed Gracie wasn't wearing her *la* Baby Doll sweatshirt.

She was trying to look sexy, and the guys were noticing her. The dogs were checking her out. She had on a lot of make-up, including red lipstick and blue eye shadow, and wore a low-cut blouse that showed her child's cleavage and the trim of her push-up bra. She wore tight pants with her belly exposed.

As Noni handed Equis a crumbled ten-dollar bill, Gracie watched her, like she was looking through the window of a pastry shop. "Give me a hit," said the dead woman.

"I got something to show you," I said to Gracie.

"Don't go with him," said the dead woman.

"Not now, okay, Victor? Maybe later, okay?"

"Come on. It won't take long."

Reluctantly, she seemed to pull her eyes away from her sister's transaction. "Okay, what?"

"Damn!" said Equis to Noni, watching Gracie's butt as she walked away. "Your little sister's looking hot tonight."

I brought her into my room and told her to sit on the mattress. Like a rebellious kid who didn't want to do what her parents told her, she sat down, arms crossed.

"This is a complete waste of time," said the dead woman.

I got my pencil and pad.

"You gonna draw me right now?" Gracie said standing up. "I don't want to right now, okay?"

"Come on," I said. "Just a quickie, okay? Please, sit down. It's important. Please trust me."

I heard Equis outside laughing. "Did you hear that? They're having a quickie."

"Come on," I said. "Sit down, please?"

She sat down. The dead lady was behind her. I drew her eyes, her nose, her mouth. I drew her gently, slowly and made her look peaceful. I drew her hair, long strokes of the pencil, her hair so full. I added shadow on one side of her face, and shaded her eyelids.

"What's your name?" I asked, without looking up.

"Claire," she said.

"You know my name!" said Gracie. "Where's your brain?"

I don't know how long the drawing took, but it must have been a while, because *la* Baby Doll had dozed off and was lying on the mattress in a curled up position. The lady was sitting there, so radiant, so peaceful, as if she were listening to great music.

"Do you want to see it?" I asked her.

She nodded.

I stood up and walked across the room and showed it to her.

"You're dead," I said. She looked at the picture, reached out to touch it and her hands begin to disintegrate into particles.

"What? Are you finally done?" *la* Baby Doll asked, waking up. Her voice was squeaky, like a little kid. "It's about time!"

She sat up. "Dang, that was a good nap! I can't sleep this good at home, because you never know what that pervert my mom married is going to do."

"Sleep some more if you want," I said. "There's nothing out there worth getting up for. I'll watch over you."

"I *am* kind of sleepy," she said.

"Go ahead. I'll stay here. I'll draw you sleeping."

"Dang!" she said. "You're such a good big brother." She reached up and kissed me on the cheek. Then she curled up on the mattress and fell back asleep.

☙ ☙ ☙

This party we were going to next was supposed to be a big one, a *pachanga* put on by some old guys. I don't think Equis wanted me to go, because he thought I might get into trouble and get him into trouble. I told him I was going anyway.

"All right, Victor. But don't mess with the wrong people."

"I'm not afraid of anyone."

My dad was there next to me. "Let's get in a fight tonight," he said.

Equis' ghost was next to him, some tall, skinny guy with big eyes that always looked afraid. He was wearing a space helmet made of glass. "I don't want to go," he said. "I just want to stay home in bed. Please, let's not go."

"I'm just not in a party mood, I guess," Equis said.

The two dogs came out of their room, wearing their best, creased, Ben Davis work pants and crisp, white T-shirts. "Let's party," one said, followed by three ghosts.

I rode shotgun and Equis and one of the dogs were in the back.

We were smoking, and the air smelled like skunk. The lights were blurring through the windows.

I heard laughing. Saw a light flick on above me.

"What's up, Victor?" Equis said.

I remembered those guys were surrounding me, hurting me, kicking me. I remember I felt rage, all of them kicking me, hitting me with sticks, and at the moment that I was shot, I wanted nothing more than to hurt them.

I want to kill them all. Now I found myself with my boys. We were getting out of the car. It was exciting because that night held so many possibilities. As we walked toward the house, we saw cholos on the front lawn drinking beer. When I passed through them, I thought of something.

"Whoa!" I said and stopped walking.

"What's the matter?" Equis asked.

"What if I'm dead? What if I just thought I came back to life?"

"What are you talking about?"

"What if I never made it?"

"Damn, you're stoned. Maybe we shouldn't go in."

"Look at all these clowns," I said, looking around the party at the most exaggerated cholo stereotypes you could imagine. "This ain't real. These people are too one-dimensional. How could anyone fall for this?"

"Maintain, bro. They're going to jump you."

"Is it possible I didn't survive?"

"You survived, fool. All right? Now stay right here. I'm getting you come coffee or something. Damn, you stay away from that stuff."

I started barking real loud, and some cholos wearing red, Bulldog T-shirts standing on the lawn looked at me like I was crazy. I heard a few distant barks come from other parts of the party.

Equis came toward me. "Sorry, man," he said to the cholos. "He don't know what he's doing." He pulled me aside. "Bro, what's wrong with you? You can't bark."

If I had been dead all these years since I was killed by bangers, it would explain a lot of things.

I created Ilaina. I created my cousin Johnny. I created Jessica. Everything that was happening I created.

None of this story is true.

How did I think I could survive a gun to my stomach? It's impossible.

I had been fooling myself, and maybe that was why I felt so much rage all the time. My story has been about another worthless cholo, another worthless Chicano teenager who's confused and full of rage. I'm just a dead banger. That's why everyone thinks I'm in a gang. I *was* in a gang. How else can you explain being killed *in a gang fight!*

I barked some more. Equis tried to shut me down. "Equis," I said. "I could kill you. Know why? Because you're already dead."

"Shut up, man!

We entered the house.

Someone handed me something to drink and I drank. I saw a girl sitting on a couch squeezed in with a bunch of others, but she was just looking around as if everything made her nervous. I told her to relax.

She looked around as if everything scared her. She took tiny sips from her cup of beer and winced at each taste.

I had to piss. I went down the hallway, which was filled with cholos and girls making out in the dark. I saw two guys all over one girl. I was about to see if she needed help, but then I realized that one of the guys was dead.

I went further into the hallway, and saw some of the bedroom doors were opened and people were in the rooms partying, too. I saw an old woman standing by the bed, her face all wrinkled, and she was looking down, holding a rosary in her hands mumbling a prayer for her granddaughter, who was some strung-out chola with a guy kissing her even though she looked passed out. I asked some girls if they knew where the bathroom was. They pointed to a door, but it was locked. I knocked.

"Hurry up," I said, and I knocked again.

Some guy yelled back, "Get out of here."

Then I heard a girl's voice inside. "We should go back," she said.

"No, hell, no," he said.

"I don't wanna," she said, and she sounded real young. I pictured Gracie in there, being molested by some guy.

Every Chicanita is my sister.

"Don't make me break down this door," I said, pounding on it.

The door opened and some big guy came out. He was the size of a football player, "Who said that?" he was so tall he looked over my head before he noticed me.

"That's my little sister," I said.

I kneed the guy between the legs and he fell. I kneed him on the way down, in the face. I heard something crunch and blood splattered out of his face. He fell down, out of the bathroom, against the walls of the hallway.

The girl ran down the hallway.

A dead woman with tattered clothes was sitting on the closed toilet seat, weeping.

"You're dead," I said, and she disintegrated.

I looked in the mirror. There I was, El Apache, my wide nose and dark face, my head nearly shaved. My father seemed to appear in the mirror next to me. His hair was like an afro, and he was smiling. "Let's go finish that guy off," he said.

Then I noticed a bunch of people behind me, about a hundred. They kept expanding back there, a crowd of people, way too many to count. They all looked angry, blood-thirsty, dead bikers, dead cholos, a dead cop with his Billy club drawn.

The big cholo rushed at me and pushed me into the wall. He had a knife and he stuck it in me once, and it hurt like hell but it made me feel alive. Like maybe I wasn't dead. How could the dead feel pain?

I heard voices, and I pushed him back. Then time slowed to a crawl. I put my foot behind his ankles and pushed. He fell back like a bag of cement. People were crowding into the hallway to see us, and I stomped him like a fire that needed to be put out.

�֎ ✖֎ ✖֎

On the way back home, sitting in the backseat, Equis seemed worried that I was going to die. I guess I was losing a lot of blood. He put his bandana on my stomach, and it was redder than ever.

"We should take him to a hospital."

"I'm fine," I said.

The big cholo I fought was in the backseat with me. "Let's go again," he said.

"Oh, just shut up," I said. "You're dead. I killed you."

"Man, there's something wrong with your head," Equis said. "You better lay off the *mota.*"

"No, not you. Him."

"Do you know whose house that was?" Equis asked.

The guys stopped at a drugstore and got bandages and alcohol. That night someone took care of me. I don't know who, but it was some girl, or I dreamed her. She was with me, and every time I woke up she was there.

"What's your name," I asked,

She nodded her head, as if it were a silly question.

"What's your name?"

"It's still Marianne," she said.

"I like that name," I said.

"You should like it," she said.

"Sometimes I think I'm dead."

"Get some sleep. You need rest."

"It's just that . . ." I looked around.

I fell asleep again.

※ ※ ※

I dreamed that I was jumped by the gang of the dead. They surrounded me, hundreds of them, and they beat me over and over again. Incredibly, there was something soothing about their kicks and punches, as if I were being rocked in a cradle.

When I woke up it was daytime. I sat up, and looked around for Marianne.

I got up and walked out of the bedroom. The guys were sitting around talking. Equis saw me and said, "You must have an angel watching over you!" he said.

"You mean Marianne?"

"Who?" he asked.

"That girl."

"That girl? Turns out that she was the little sister of the *veterano* throwing the party. You're his favorite person in the world right now. You're like a hero now."

"Lucky!" one of the guys said.

"They want to have a meeting with us," said Equis.

"What do you mean? What girl did I save? Marianne? Is she still here?"

"What's he talking about?" someone asked.

And I heard their voices, but I wasn't paying attention to who was saying what, because I was looking around for something. I was going to do something, and that's why I walked out of the bedroom, but now I couldn't remember what I was looking for.

"Don't you remember anything about last night?"

"He was *all* messed up!"

"Remember the fight?"

"The girl you saved from being raped."

"Where is the girl?" I insisted.

"She's not here."

"She's Mando's sister."

"You know who he is?"

"I think you should just kill yourself."

"Victor, what do you remember from last night?"

I remembered only a light, walking into the party, walking into the light.

Over time, they would tell me the details, and I would remember things from that night at random times. Eventually I remembered the fight. I thought I killed him, but he was just beat up.

I was *all* messed up.

Here's the facts:

The *veteranos* were grateful that I took care of the rapist. They cared that I was the son of Victor Reyes, and they told me that I was just like him. Then they got down to business. My pot business.

They wanted in. Instead of selling small amounts of pot to casual smokers, they wanted me to deal in larger amounts, larger accounts and let others do the small stuff. The pot business they told me had suffered in California, because many people who used to buy from dealers now got it legally. However, Fresno was a politically conservative county, as was the entire San Joaquin Valley, and there were few legal dispensaries like there were in LA and San Francisco. They would finance me, but it would be my operation. All I had to do was pay them 20% of my profits.

They handed me a roll of cash and gave me the contact information, and the next thing you know I was buying ten pounds of high-grade stuff from some gangster-looking Assyrian dudes, the most pot I had ever seen in one place. They were new to the business, so they were giving me a huge discount.

They had it in the back of their car wrapped tightly in plastic. One of them wore a tight, white sweater, a gold chain and a lot of cologne. After our transaction, he gave me a cool, handshake slide and thanked me.

I visited La Abuela. When she let me into her house, she asked me how much I wanted. I told her I wanted to talk business. I asked how much she got at one time and what she paid. Before I left there, I became her new supplier. She bought a brick. I was able to return their investment within a week, so other than the twenty percent, from now on, the rest of the money was for me.

I kept about five grand in a shoebox in my room, which was formerly Equis' room, but now he slept on the couch. I showed him where I kept the stash, stuffed inside a hole in the mattress.

"I want you to sell little bags. This is where I keep it."

"What do I do with your cash?" he asked.

"You put it in. . . . " I looked around, trying to remember where I hid a box of cash. "Shit. I had a box of *feria* somewhere. I don't remember where I put it."

"How much was in there?" he asked.

"About five grand."

"And you lost it?"

"No, it's somewhere. Oh yeah," I said and I looked in the closet, way on top and pulled out a shoebox. I opened it, but there were pens and charcoals, no money. "What did I do with it?"

"You're *all* messed up."

"Oh, yeah! The washing machine out back. If you stick your hands inside, you'll feel a big coffee can. Put the money in there."

"Damn!" he said. "That don't seem like a very good hiding place. You need to hide it somewhere good."

"That's just the cash box," I said. "I hid the real cash all around the city. In places no one'll ever find."

"I hope you wrote it down like a treasure map," said Equis. "Knowing you, you'll forget."

"I'll remember. I got four or five, or . . . I think I'll remember all of them."

✹ ✹ ✹

One night, we were all partying in the living room. There were a bunch of us, boys and girls.

Equis and I were arguing about some dumb stuff that didn't matter, like who was hotter, Cristina Aguilera or Shakira, something stupid like that, and I forgot what it was about and so I just called him an idiot. Everyone else was watching us, and Equis was on that night, making everyone laugh. "Hey, Victor, you forgot what we were talking about, didn't you? Did you remember you're my bitch?"

Everyone laughed.

I looked at the door. I was expecting someone to come in.

"You going to let him call you that?" someone said.

"Shh! Someone's at the door," I said.

"Who's here?"

"He's hoping it's his hoochie mama," Equis said. "*La* Baby Doll."

"Someone should go check," I said. "We should be keeping it locked now."

The front door opened, and it was Noni and Gracie, and they came in and the party kept going, but I kept looking at the door.

"What's got you all paranoid?" Gracie asked.

I was still looking at the door, expecting to see someone come in.

"Can I get some weed from you?" she asked.

"What? You smoke weed now?"

"I don't do that other shit," she said.

I wanted to say, Gracie, I'm disappointed in you, but I knew she was the same age as I was when I started smoking pot.

Equis came up and told Gracie to follow him, and I wanted to tell her about the adolescent brain and pot, but he lead her to the bedroom to let her pick out a bag. I just watched them, and I wanted to stop them, but I felt like I needed to be near the door.

And someone did come through the front door.

They came in from the backdoor too, knocking it down. They had rifles and helmets and they told us to get on the floor face down.

They couldn't hold me for long.

There was no evidence that I even lived in the house. It had been rented under someone else's name, so as far as the police knew, I was just another one of the guys partying there, and there were a lot of us that night, about 30. I had nothing on me when they threw me on the ground and frisked me, so they couldn't get me on possession or dealing. I had no identification, having left all my personal stuff at Jessica's, so I told them my name was Juan García and that I was 21, and they didn't seem to care if I was lying. They had bigger things to go after.

Like Equis. I would find out later that it didn't go so well for him. He had some meth in his pocket, and a whole lot of marijuana. He also had hidden in the closet his identification, his birth certificate. When they stormed the house, he had his knife on him, and he was so good at opening and closing it that he had instinctively pulled it from his pocket, opened it and lunged at a cop and cut him on the arm. They pinned the drugs on him and charged him with attempted murder of a police officer.

But the worst part of it was Gracie, her first arrest: possession of marijuana and underage drinking. They even tried to pin some meth charges on her, since she was in the bedroom with Equis.

Eventually, they would let her go, as it was a first offense and she was only fourteen years old. I knew this kind of experience would mark her for life, being frisked, thrown into a cell, watching the police round up her own sister, grab her by the neck and throw her into the back of a police van. I knew her life would be different. Her eyes would be less wide.

My mind had been so numb from smoking and partying that I allowed someone I cared for to be put in that situation. In fact, two days in the jail cell gave me two days of sobriety, and the clarity came back immediately.

I knew I needed to stop.

In my mind I had pictured myself as some character on the TV show *Weeds*, innocently selling pot to my neighbors, but it was an illegal business and people died.

If they were encroaching on someone else's territory, those two Assyrian guys could be dead by now. And I knew that those who sold pot also sold meth and *chiva*, and I was no different from them.

I knew I needed to do something positive with the cash I had hidden around the city. I just didn't know what.

※ ※ ※

When I left the jail, I was hungry. I walked through the downtown, outdoor mall where Mexicans shopped, and there were *cholitos* riding their lowrider bikes, old men sitting on the benches and talking, and a preacher holding up a Bible and saving souls in Spanish. I smelled the hotdogs a street vendor was hocking. I wanted one, but I didn't have any money on me.

My stomach felt bad, like it hurt from being empty. The smell of the hotdogs in the cart was so good.

I thought about going home to Jessica, but I figured I had burnt that bridge. If she found out that I was just another cholo in a drug bust, it would confirm all she had believed about me.

She had been right about me all along. I was determined to be the stereotype that fit me best, the one that was the easiest for me to be. I was just another branch on the cholo tree.

Then I remembered Mr. García's place. It was summer, so he was in San Francisco, and if he still had the key under the rock on the side of the house, I could go in there and eat. Then I would I get out of Fresno and start a new life.

I would walk along some railroad tracks, maybe jump on a train to who knows where, into a new place, a new universe. Maybe I would start a legal business, like an art supply store, and in the evenings I could give drawing lessons to the kids in the neighborhood.

At Mr. García's house I knocked over and over without an answer. I was certain that he was gone for the summer. I walked to the side of the house, and found the rock. The key was there, so I took it and went to the door. I hoped the neighbors didn't think much of a cholo entering his house, but they had seen me before so often, or should have, the days I used to come over and paint.

I went into the house. All the blinds were closed, and it was dim and cool. I left the lights off. The other side of the house, facing the backyard, was a wall of bay windows. You could see the garden and the square of green lawn. There was also a bunch of lawn furniture out there: a table, some empty chairs and empty recliners.

I went to the kitchen. It was so quiet in there that my footsteps seemed to echo. I stopped to listen. I could hear a distant leaf blower and the sound of children some-where far off, yelling and laughing. Their voices played in the air and then were sucked in and vanished, like ghosts trapped in another world. I could hear myself breathing. I started to feel a little scared, like I was in a haunted house. Just to make sure that I was alone, I went from room to room checking everything. I entered Mr. García's bedroom, and it looked so neat, so perfect, so clean and arranged. The tan carpet was clean and shiny, like in a new home. The bed was made, a big bed high from the ground with a white comforter and big, white pillows. There were windows on both sides of it, white curtains, white blinds shut tight. Still, enough sun came in to light up the place, and the white comforter shined.

Everything was quiet except for that distant leaf blow-er. Suddenly, the distant voices and laughter of children faded in again, and then it faded out again just as fast.

I looked under the bed, just to be sure there were no crazy axe murderers under there.

"No ghosts here," I said aloud.

I walked to each of the rooms and checked them. In one room he had set up his office. There was a desk and a computer and some bookshelves. I looked in the closet. In another bedroom all he had was an exercise bike and a weight set that probably hadn't been used since he had bought it. I looked in that closet too. It was full of clothes and boxes, but no axe murderers.

When I reached the room at the end of the hallway, I found it was locked. At first I panicked, because I thought that if it was locked then someone must have been in there, but then I remembered that it was Mr. García's pri-vate room, and he always kept it locked. He had told me he kept his old paintings and art stuff in there.

I wondered what kind of stuff he used to paint, and I was about to force my way in, just to see his paintings. But something stopped me, maybe some sense of mystery that I held within me about what I would see. Sometimes the power of mystery is knowing that you'll never know what it truly means. I pictured myself looking through his paintings, but I couldn't imagine what he would have painted, what images would have mattered to him, so I saw myself going through piles of canvases, the light of unseen images shining on my face.

I went to the kitchen. I looked in the refrigerator. There wasn't much in there, just some jars of pickles and condiments and a few six packs of soda.

But the freezer was like a treasure of goodies, frozen lasagna, meat, fish sticks, all kinds of munchies, including ice cream and popsicles.

In the pantry I found cans of beans, meat, soups and I found pastas, pancake mix, a bunch of good stuff.

Cans of food had never looked so inviting.

I decide to cook a meal and pig out something serious.

I started cooking pasta and all kinds of stuff. The Italian chef, Mario, came back. "We is a-cooking again!" he said in his exaggerated Italian accent. "Mama mia!"

"Hand me the oregano," I said to him.

When I woke up it was dark.

I thought I was dreaming.

A loud noise.

A deafening squeal, like screeching metal, swirled in the blackness, and it reverberated throughout my head and into my bones.

I held my palms to my ears and fell off the couch onto the floor. I tried to hide from whatever it was, which turned out to be the automatic sprinklers.

I fell back asleep and a bunch of cholo ghouls were coming after me. I curled my body into a little ball, as if I were protecting myself from kicks. Their shadowy figures surrounded me. There were three of them. Or four. They were kicking me in the ribs, on the head, on my back. I saw light flash on one of their faces, a Cholo Frankenstein kicking me over and over in rage and hatred. One of them had a stick and he beat me with it. And then I saw the shotgun.

Something was waiting for me in a tunnel, waiting to pull me in, and I was sucked into a wormhole.

I was maybe two years old.

We were in the front yard of our house, and it was nice and sunny. I heard birds singing in the treetops. My mother was sitting on the steps, and I was walking around on the small patch of front lawn. I was just a little kid, barely learning to walk. I walked with my arms opened for balance.

My father was working on his car in the driveway, a 1976 Monte Carlo. The door handles were gone, because he was going to install automatic buttons. He had been working on it most of my life with him—a job he would never finish. Years after he died, Jessica still had that car. To open the doors, she had to stick her short fingers into the holes and pull a wire.

I was walking on the lawn trying to keep my balance, trying to stay on my feet.

I saw my father sanding down the holes on the doors, and my mother clapped her hands and I began to turn around so I could see her. I could barely control my movements, so turning around wasn't easy. I had to walk laterally, so I could point my head and body in her direction.

I saw the world spin by, blurred, like a half turn of a merry-go-round, but it was the world, the entire world spinning.

When I stopped moving, I was facing my mother, but I was losing balance. I saw young Jessica sitting on those steps. Her hair was up. She was smiling at me, and I lost balance and fell on my butt. She laughed and said, "Oh, no!"

I was on Mr. García's floor.

I remembered what happened when I died.

I see it like a scene from a corny movie.

There *was* a great, white light. My father walked out of it. He was covered with light like a cholo angel, a white bandana tied around his head. He was standing in the light, opposite me. He walked toward me, held out his hand to me. He said something to me. Maybe, he said. "*M'ijo,* do you want another chance at life?" Or maybe he said, "*M'ijo,* I love you and will always be with you."

Maybe all he said was *M'ijo.*

Maybe he said, "Paint me."

"Paint me."

He wanted me to paint him.

I went into the studio and turned on the lights. My paintings were still there. The one on the easel was of Iliana. She was sitting in the garden. She was looking at me like she still loved me.

The studio had a wall of windows looking onto the backyard. I could see a sprinkler slowly spinning, like the second hand of a clock, and the water dripping from leaves and rocks. I saw my own full-body reflection in the window. I stood there looking at me, like in a mirror, but it was a window so you could see through me, to the yard. My reflection walked away from itself, and it appeared on the other side of the glass. Out there, it became my father. He was outside, standing underneath a fruit tree, looking at me. It was him. I walked closer to the glass to get a better look. I flicked on a porch light and his body started to dissolve into particles of light. They floated around and landed on everything, on an empty lawn chair, a tree, the grass. My father was the chair. My father was a perfect square of lawn. My father was the orange tree, yellow flowers, the wooden fence.

I set up an easel with a fresh canvas and, deciding on oils, I set up the paints, the linseed oil, the turpentine.

I started with smooth strokes of green, slashing the white flesh of the canvas.

I remembered *The Rite of Spring*.

I put down the brush and went to the stereo, looked for the Stravinsky and put it on.

I went back to the canvas and painted, playing *The Rite of Spring* over and over again. The sprinklers were off, and the place was silent and cool the way mornings can be cool. I stepped into the next room and rested on the couch and fell asleep again.

I woke up to the sound of a motor.

I sat up and saw that the gardeners were outside. There were three of them. They were short and dark, and they yelled back and forth to each other in Hmong. One of them wore a red cap.

I stood up and went to see what I had painted.

You could tell it was a garden if you stood far away, but from up close, it looked like chaos.

I started working on it again, making the edges of things a little sharper, so the image could appear more real. Reality was sharp, memory was soft, muted. Death was soft. Life was hard.

I didn't want the painting to be realistic. I wanted more of an impressionistic look, an explosion of blurry colors making up an image, the way the world looks to a spinning child. But the more I painted, guided by the brush and the lines, the more things became sharp.

I ended up putting the three gardeners in the painting. I did one of them pushing the lawn mower. One of them, I put trimming the rose bushes with shears. The one with the red cap was rolling up a green garden hose.

I didn't care if the workers saw me, because I knew they would think I was a guest of Mr. García's.

At one point I even went out there with cold sodas and handed one to each of them. They said thanks.

I told them that if they were hungry, let me know, I'd cook something for them.

I painted all day and into the night. I stopped only to eat and for other necessities. I listened to Stravinsky, but I also listened to Oldies like War and El Chicano, stuff my father used to like, Led Zeppelin and Pink Floyd. I listened to Death Metal.

The muted colors and soft edges I thought would be impressionistic turned out to be sharp edges. And things were stark, realistic. The image of the backyard was almost like a photo.

But without having realized it, I had painted the image broken up into shards, like a broken mirror on which reality was reflected. Only the shards made up a clear image, because between them I put muted colors and curves and shapes. I put light and swirls of color and sounds.

In the yard, I painted the three gardeners, but I also added Jessica and Mr. García and Equis. I put in Gracie. I put me out there painting, all of us standing around in the backyard, like a gathering of souls.

I looked at the painting and realized that none of the people were talking to each other or even looking at each other. They looked like the disconnected people in a David Hockney painting. It was like everyone was in the same place, but everyone was by his or herself. No one was together.

But between the shards, in those swirls of color and light, everything was moving together, like swirls of energy. Everything was connected.

I called the painting, *When We Were Talking in the Garden*. Even though my father wasn't one of the people inside, I knew it was a painting of him.

Someone rang the doorbell.

Without thinking about it, as if I were in my own home, I walked to the door and answered.

There were two cops standing there.

"Do you live here?" one of them asked.

I had been sitting in the cell for a full day when a guard came and opened it. He yelled my last name and pointed for me to get out. I stood up and walked out. After he closed the door I followed him down the hallway. He was a white guy with red hair and freckles. He twirled his nightstick like a cop on the beat. We passed doors and cells with a bunch of tough-looking guys in orange jumpsuits. I guess I hadn't been there long enough to get one of those outfits.

"Where are you taking me?" I asked.

"You got a visitor," he said.

We walked out into an open area. Standing there, arms crossed like he was angry, was Mr. García. They must have called him and told him that some cholo was robbing his house. He looked pissed. As I approached him, I held my head down a bit, as if I was sorry for what I had done. He saw me, shook his head in disappointment and said, "Let's go."

We walked out of the station, into the hot night. We were walking to his car, none of us saying a thing. You could hear a few car horns honking from far off.

I thought I had better say something. "I'm sorry," I said.

"I am so angry," he said.

"I know, I'm . . . "

He interrupted. "How dare they arrest you. They come to *my* house and arrest *my* guest? I tell you right now, Victor, I never wanted to believe it, but I think it's because you're Hispanic."

"Uh, yeah," I said. "So you're not mad at me?"

"Mad at you? What for?"

"For coming into your house."

A cop car pulled up to the front of the station, and two cops pulled out a Chicano man, a cholo-looking guy, and they dragged him through the double doors. The cholo was yelling stuff to them about *innocence* and *stupid*.

As I stood there watching, I couldn't help but wonder: What if I could see something and paint it right away? How many paintings would I do each hour, just being in the city? I'd paint that cholo being dragged to jail by the police. I didn't care if the art schools didn't like me paint-ing cholos. I'd paint them anyway.

"I said you could come by and paint whenever you wanted, Victor."

"Uh, thanks."

"They had no right to arrest you."

"I ate all your food."

I looked up into the sky. You couldn't see a single star, just color and the dim glow of the city.

"Oh, and that painting you just did is beautiful. It's like a Picasso and hyperrealism and Impressionism all in one. I love what's between those cracks of glass. Those shapes. Victor, can I ask you something?"

"Of course."

"Did you put another world inside those cracks? When I look at it, I can swear I see something."

"What do you see?" I asked.

"A city."

"I didn't put it there," I said.

"Oh, yes you did."

"You imagined it."

"You painted something that caused me to imagine it. No matter what I imagine I see in the cracks of that image, no matter what other universes I got a glimpse of, you provided the opportunity for me to see it. That's what an artist does. *Sees.* And teaches us to see. Did you know that when some people look at a Jackson Pollock painting they see a bunch of horse heads and hidden faces?"

His car was parked on the street, under a tree.

"So you're not mad that I ate all your food?"

"I tell you what I'm peeved about. Those idiots arrest-ing you." He stopped walking, and he grabbed me by my shoulders and looked me in the eyes. The city was shining in his eyes. "Did they mistreat you in anyway?"

"No, not really, I mean, you know, they're cops."

"What do you mean?"

"They're not cruise directors, you know?"

He started walking again.

"Well I'm going to file a complaint, you can bet on that. I'm also a little peeved at you, Mr. Reyes." He pressed the button on his key chain and his car beeped and the lights flashed on. They shined right on us, our shadows stretching behind us like spirits were following us. "I'm perturbed that you didn't apply to the school in Paris."

We got into the car.

I strapped myself into the passenger's seat. "What for?"

"Quit whining," he said. "Besides, I did it for you. I already thought about it, and I don't want you so say anything right now, but if you get in, I'm going to lend you the money."

"You wouldn't have to do that. I'd find a way."

"It won't be cheap."

He pulled onto the street, and we were driving back to his house.

EPILOGUE

The directions to the school were easy to follow.

I got off the plane, followed the lights to customs, *Douane*, and then I found the train and bought a ticket from the machine.

I sat on the train leaving the airport. We shot into a dark tunnel.

I looked at the other passengers, and many of them were black and brown people. When the train shot out of the tunnel, we were sliding through the suburbs. Some of the stops we made along the way seemed to be in poor parts of the city, and there were a lot of black people. That made me feel a little more comfortable, because my image was that I would enter the city, me, a cholo with baggy pants, a Chicano in Paris, and all the white people would stare at me and say, *"Mon dieu! Qu'est-ce que c'est?"*

But I felt pretty good, like I belonged. There were a lot of watermelon people. You couldn't tell what ethnicity they were, but they were brown.

Some of them were Algerian, Moroccan, Lebanese, but they weren't all Arabs like the US media showed them. Some of the young people were second- or third-generation French, and they dressed like cholos too, baggy pants, caps pulled back, big football T-shirts with numbers on them. A lot of the young, African men were total hip hop, some of them wearing pants so baggy that they hung down past their boxers. Some of the brown and black boys, seeing the way I was dressed, even nodded to me.

On the train, there was a brown kid, about fifteen years old, sitting across from me. He was listening to his smart phone. He was shaking his head, *all* into the music. He had baggy pants and was all gangsta looking. I wanted to draw him, because he could have been a boy in Fresno. The only difference was that in the windows around his shoulders the suburbs of Paris were streaming by like a silent film.

I pulled the sketchpad out of my backpack and sketched him. I tried not to look at him too much, because I didn't want him to know I was drawing him. I sketched quickly, but I guess people couldn't help it. If someone was near enough to look at my pad, they looked. They saw who I was drawing and they looked at him and then at the drawing again.

The train stopped in a neighborhood surrounded by projects where poor people must have lived. More people got on. A thin, black man sat right next to me. He wore a fedora hat, something a grandfather would wear. He was pretty old, maybe in his fifties.

They nodded at me, as if to say, *Good day*. He had big cheeks and big eyes. He looked at my pad and then at the boy sitting across the train.

He said something to me in French, which I assumed was something about being an artist. I heard the word *artiste*.

"I'm sorry," I said. "I don't speak French."

"English?" he asked me.

"Yeah." I nodded. "Or Spanish."

"Mexico?" he said.

"Yeah, sort of," I said.

He pointed at the pen drawing of the boy on my pad. "You are very good."

I shrugged. "Thanks," I said.

The train went into another tunnel, and the city disappeared. The windows became black. The train shook as it moved along.

"I'm here to study," I said.

He nodded.

"Can I draw you?" I asked.

"Me?" He laughed, as if he wasn't worthy of being drawn. "Go ahead. Be my friend."

So I drew him.

Other passengers looked over at us and watched his face and upper body appear in black ink on the white page.

Then the train came to another stop and the voice announced, *Chatalet.*

The doors slid open.

I showed him the drawing and then put it into my backpack.

I stood up.

"Thanks. It was nice talking to you," I said.

We both stepped out of the train, into the station. Thousands of people were going all directions, to other trains and to subways, and I saw a sign that said, *Sortie,* Exit, *Salida.*

"God bless you," he said.

"Thanks," I said, and he left.

As he left, I saw the top of his head disappear into a sea of bodies.

I stood there amazed at all the people, thousands and thousands. I had my backpack and a suitcase on wheels. People blurred by as if they were in a hurry, women with fancy purses and high-heeled shoes, men talking on cell phones, teenage boys with earphones pumping high energy music into their heads—a blur of countless people. Across the station, on the other side of the tracks, some Peruvian or Bolivian musicians were playing guitars and flutes.

Against one wall, I saw an old, Arab lady on her knees. She was sitting on a small blanket begging for money, a cup in front of her. When a passerby put coins in her cup, she swayed her body up and down as if she were praying. I looked in my pockets, but all I could find was a ten Euro note, which was about fifteen dollars. I walked over to her blanket. I put the ten Euros in her cup. She swayed back and forth and mumbled some blessing in Arabic.

Also by Daniel Chacón

and the shadows took him, A Novel
Chicano, Chicanery
Hotel Juárez: Stories, Rooms and Loops
Unending Rooms